DE 12 12

LIFE SENTENCE

LIFE SENTENCE

OLGA HESKY

c.4

PUBLISHED FOR THE CRIME CLUB BY
DOUBLEDAY & COMPANY, INC.
GARDEN CITY, NEW YORK
1972

DB — 11-22-72 — CRIME CLUB 2.75

All of the characters in this book
are fictitious, and any resemblance
to actual persons, living or dead,
is purely coincidental.

First Edition

ISBN: 0-385-00090-1
Library of Congress Catalog Card Number 72–79395
Copyright © 1972 by Olga Hesky
All Rights Reserved
Printed in the United States of America

TO. THE. ONLIE. BETETTER. OF.
THIS. UNSUING. STORIE.
MR. R. FREEBAIRN-SMITH.
ALL. HAPPINESSE.

O.H.

LIFE SENTENCE

CHAPTER 1

'John Aldous Waggoner!'

The voices bellowed, hollow and sonorous, reverberating round the court, bouncing from wall to wall and among the medieval-type architraves. They were not actually calling him—he was already there—nor addressing him directly; yet the name, his own, seemed to speak itself into his heart, to identify him to himself so that briefly, in a rare and not very comfortable fashion he knew who he really was.

Of course it was partly the circumstances which made everything so strange, so weighted with consequence. Also, Waggoner explained to himself, it was hearing his middle name, Aldous. Funny how just the sound of it brought him, all of a sudden, face to face with himself as though he'd been incomplete without it, although he'd practically forgotten it, not even bothering to fill it in on all the forms and papers he'd been signing lately. Nobody used it; even the policeman hadn't when he'd read out the formal charge.

'John Waggoner,' he'd said solemnly, almost portentiously, his round, fair, youthful face quite sad. (Had he been sad? Sorry? Sorry for Waggoner?) The speculation passed light as the touch of a moth wing across the surface of Waggoner's mind before he began to wonder how they'd found out about the name.

Well, as they'd found out about everything, about his entire life, it appeared, from all sorts of documents: birth certificate, marriage licence, insurance cards, all that. . . . They'd dug up much that Waggoner himself had long forgotten and had never considered either important or interesting.

Still, the fact that the policeman hadn't used his full proper name might make a difference; might make the whole thing, the whole trial illegal, mightn't it?

Waggoner had heard of cases where formalities and technicalities ignored or mis-used had had a supreme power, like the waving of a magic wand, changing everything, cancelling everything. He nodded and scribbled down the words: *'Missing name; identity doubtful? Grounds for appeal?'* on the pad thoughtfully provided.

He folded the note, intending to have it passed to Mr. Fifterley. But stopped, remembering in time—before making a fool of himself—that he didn't want an appeal unless he could be sure it would be refused after an interesting and comfortable waste of time.

But, he thought, firming his chin, there was a right and a wrong way of doing things. To deprive a man of part of his own name (especially at such a climactic point in his life) must be wrong. Even though they gave the name back later. . . .

'John Aldous Waggoner.' They were at it again. It was funny to think that Andy, who, when all was said and done, had been the central figure in Waggoner's life of late, had probably never even known about this singular and singularizing middle name. . . . Andy who had lived and died with and (in a sense) for him. Andy, but for whom.

It was also strange to think that there was no one left to call him anything but Waggoner—or Mr. Waggoner! No one would tell you himself that he was not a smiling type. Laugh, instead: something like, for instance 563287, say. There was no reason why he wouldn't get used to it, maybe even prefer it to a name. Waggoner had never had friends—what you could call friends. He'd never had time for that sort of thing. From now on, though, he might. And they might give him a nickname, affectionately shortening his number.

'Old 87,' he could imagine them saying, 'he's all right, old 87 is, when you get to know him. Bit on the quiet side, like; but a good sort.'

It was that name business that had this effect of making him feel—sort of three-dimensional, you might call it. Like seeing another person, in a case in the papers or the sort of individual they had on the telly, being interviewed, or discussed, if it was interesting enough. It was as though he was looking at himself from outside his own skin; and that had never happened before, though he had been brought up short, surprised as it were, at the sight of himself as he talked to other people. This, too, was a new experience.

The first time it had been really funny, seeing his own picture in the paper. Afterwards he'd become increasingly indifferent, mainly because it was always the same picture. And the reason for that was that there had never been more than the one photo of him, so they'd had to use that every time.

One of them, one of those reporters must have pinched it from the house. It had always stood in the same place, on the dressing-table, at an angle on the corner. The frame might have been silver, but it was now so tarnished you couldn't tell. Agnes had put it there in the first place and had dutifully kept it there though she probably hadn't really seen it any more than Waggoner himself had. Habit had blended it into the background, the bedroom wallpaper—which had also become invisible in the same way, for the same reason, so that Waggoner really couldn't have told what the pattern was, not if they'd asked him, on oath, here.

The Waggoner in the picture was a much younger Waggoner. His nose had been less boney then—or fleshier—and his ears seemed not to protrude as much as now. But then, as now, two curved lines bracketed nostrils and mouth-corners with the ghosts of deprecating smiles, lightly sketched as though never having aspired to the full status of smiles, having been no more than the possibility of becoming them. It was as if Waggoner—the pictured as well as the real one—had been waiting all these years: face all prepared, muscles at the ready until called upon to perform a smile which would appease or placate.

Waggoner had done his share of placatory smiling, but he would tell you himself that he was not a smiling type. Laugh, yes; sometimes he did, at the telly. He could be taken unawares by laughter at the downright comic—the pratfall, the foreseeable mishap when it happened as he had expected. But smile: no.

3

Not very often. The proceedings today had made him smile more than was usual with him.

Of course in the photo he had had more hair than now; but the peculiar thing was that it was parted in the middle. Waggoner knew he'd never worn a centre-parting. Had it been some passing vanity? Or had it been at the photographer's bidding? He wasn't given to vanity and couldn't imagine how this had come about. It was a minor, even a quite irrelevant point. But in all the years, all the thousands of times he had passed that photo (getting dressed or undressed, going to his side of the bed or leaving it) Waggoner had never wondered about the matter before. And it was too late now. Agnes might have been able to tell him, for she was apt to know such things, having, he supposed, little else to think about. But now he would never know the answer to that riddle.

Agnes: good and faithful to the last.

But no; not to the last, for in dying she had betrayed him. All his troubles were due to that, all his distress. It was extraordinary that this ultimate betrayal of hers should have existed in embryo all these years, unsuspected; by herself, probably, as well as by him.

Waggoner knew that it wasn't fair, really, to blame Agnes, unless you said that the whole person must be responsible for every separate part of himself, the good with the bad. It was Agnes' weakness that had betrayed them both, then; Agnes to death and Waggoner himself to—well, to life, he supposed.

He found that they were all staring at him, and he realised that he had been asked a question. They had spoken directly to him, for the first time. And instead of answering he smiled.

He was smiling not, as they might have supposed, in contempt, with intent to insult or provoke; but at the bitter irony of the question he was now being asked and which he must answer in direct opposition to his will and intent.

'Not guilty, my lord,' Waggoner said.

There were other and more subtle ironies. To be presented, as it were, with a new facet, or at least with a new view of his own personality, was a bonus Waggoner had not expected; he

4

hadn't, in fact, ever given thought to the matter or known that the need had existed. Neither self-identification nor lack of it had ever bothered him because he had always taken himself for granted. In the same way everything else, everything around him, was what he knew it to be, just as Waggoner was Waggoner.

Naturally he had had problems; but they had been of the normal, practical kind, connected with the simple mechanics of living and its minor comforts and conveniences. For example, there had been some nuisance which had worried him for a while, about the roof leaking. When it rained there had been drips and even trickles of water on the upstairs landing and it had been a long time and taken a lot of trouble until They had sent to replace the missing roof tiles. They hadn't wanted to do it, taking refuge in a variety of excuses and then in plain delays. But Agnes (that had been, of course, in good old Agnes' golden days) had kept on at Them until in the end it had all been put right.

Waggoner had a habit occasionally of putting his thoughts into rhyme. These seemed to sum up and round off a set of ideas, as though they'd been indexed, catalogued, stapled, and tied; perhaps it was a result of Waggoner's occupation: he was a filing clerk. Now he hummed silently—at the point just at the top of his nose, where all the rhymes went on:

> In good old Agnes' golden days
> They knew just what our rights meant
> Repair the holes upon the roof
> And flooding in the basement.

There hadn't really been any flooding in the basement of their house: there was no basement. Still, Waggoner needed the word to rhyme and was sure Agnes would have had that put right too if necessary.

Agnes, he had had time to find out when she was no longer there, must have been a good manager. They had never had any money to spare yet she must have known how to make it go round. In spite of rising prices, inflation, all that sort of thing, and the fact that his salary hadn't gone up at all, Waggoner had never felt any pinch then. Even Andy had done quite well and hadn't bothered Waggoner with complaints or requests, so that

5

he'd only come to realise what keeping house and buying food meant in the last terrible year.

Of course Andy had had nothing else to do; and Agnes, who was sensible and practical—qualities inherited from Andy, very likely—could contrive to buy as many kippers and sausages with the same money, even if the price went up. You could get a cheaper quality, Waggoner supposed, walk a bit farther and buy from a market or find a cut-price shop. There must be ways, and Agnes would have known them. Unfortunately, not to bother Waggoner with tales of her difficulties, she had never spoken of them, nor her ways of overcoming them.

For a novice shopper like himself, handicapped too with lack of time, such trivia had combined to build mountainous obstacles against which he had battered in vain. Waggoner pictured a great barrier formed of a myriad pebbles, each a tiny, tormenting quandary. After Agnes' death he had, in a sense, become buried beneath such a mountain, made up of kippers and sausages, of un- mended socks, of tins battered and spoilt in the opening, of unemptied garbage pails and grease-encrusted pans; and in the end there were all the disgusting chores that became worse and more impossible the longer they crouched there in the house, stinking and sneering, lying in wait for him. . . .

Waggoner smiled again, at himself this time—indulgently, pity- ingly. It had taken him quite a long time to find how to burrow out from under that mountain, how to extricate himself from it all. . . .

There was a gentle touch on his elbow. Mr. Harris, the thin reedy warder on his right, whispered in his ear. 'You may sit down.'

Waggoner felt the edge of the seat pressed solicitously, carefully, at the back of his knees. They were always careful with him and gentle and they would see that nothing hurt him or presented him difficult problems ever again.

He settled gratefully in the chair. There would be no need for him to speak again, he knew; no need to listen, even, unless he wanted. Soon it would all be over and little remained to be undergone but the boredom of formalities.

The clock high on the panelled wall above the judge's head

already said ten-thirty. The presence of the judge in scarlet robes and wig, all this panoply of bewigged and accoutred lawyers, all this reverent hush and stylized posturing and proclaiming of oaths, was all waste. A waste of the taxpayers' good money.

The tide of indignation which rose automatically in Waggoner's waste-conscious breast at this thought was swamped almost immediately by the realization that he himself, at least, would not be contributing any more to this or similar nonsense. So let the complaisant idiots pay! He, instead, would reap benefits.

He understood now, as he had never troubled to understand before, what the people meant who talked on telly about dropping out of society, or 'opting out' if they thought it was right. Well, they were on the right track, Waggoner knew; but you had to know *how*. You had to know how to opt to the border-line, so that, in fact you were opting *in!*

Naturally, this discovery, or invention, if you wanted to call it that, of Waggoner, wasn't obvious, or everybody would be doing it, and then the whole system, the system by which everything ran, was run, would just collapse.

The clues were there as soon as one knew to look for them. After which it remained only to make the logical deductions, as Waggoner had been clever enough to do. Although he admitted that but for the force of circumstances he'd probably have gone to the end of his days without catching on; as most people did.

CHAPTER 2

The lawyers were muttering among themselves and their black gowns fluttered like the feathers of angry crows. The words, multiplied and interwoven by their own echoes in arches and recesses, in the well of the court and the ceiling vaultings, became entwined, folded, pleated, and interleaved, like layers of delicate pastry separated by cream: a confection of decorous decorative ritual which no outsider such as Waggoner could hope to understand.

Not, of course, that he hoped or wished to do so. He was concerned only with the final outcome, which had always been inevitable in spite of what Mr. Fifterley, Q.C., had said. In spite, too, of what he was now saying, in full spate, stately and well-rounded phrases to the effect that his client, the accused, John Aldous Waggoner, was innocent; but that, if he had done the deed as charged, then he had meant no harm; and further that any harm he might have done, if with intent, then the intent had been sudden, spontaneous, without forethought and on irresistible impulse. He further intended to prove, Mr. Fifterley said, that Waggoner was not, and had not at any time been responsible for his actions.

Waggoner had not chosen Mr. Fifterley as his counsel. He had been chosen, presumably, by Mr. Nowditch, the solicitor. Waggoner had not chosen him, either. He had been allotted, as it were, by the Legal Aid people to Waggoner. From the beginning he'd disliked Mr. Fifterley. Nothing he could lay his finger on; just that he was like a foreigner might have been to Waggoner: outside the range of the kind of people he was accustomed to, whose reactions and responses and words-to-come he could expect—from some pattern of facial movements just as,

9

they say, animals converse with twitches of whisker and tail, flicker of eye or vellication of nose and muzzle.

The lawyer's face seemed to have been designed rather than grown in normal fashion. It was extremely red and shining as though parboiled, though his hands were very white and densely freckled. He had a disconcerting habit of speaking loudly and with exaggerated distinctness even to a single listener and another, in court, of poking vigorously beneath his wig with a gesture of exasperation. Waggoner wondered why, since his own hair was thick, curly, and ginger-grey, he didn't simply grow it to the requisite length and do without a wig altogether.

Waggoner understood that both Nowditch and Fifterley would have a vested interest in stretching out the time spent in court. They would be paid by time, he supposed, and not on results. No dog in the manger, he had no objection to that—it wasn't his money.

But a man had to think of himself and Waggoner was keen to have all this over and done with as soon as possible. He was getting very tired of the remand prison, where he was expected, even forced, to make decisions. ('What would you like for supper, Mr. Waggoner? Haddock or eggs and chips?') It was almost as tiresome as it had been at home, always having to make up his mind about food in advance, though of course he didn't have to face the lopsided piles of unwashed dishes afterwards, the stink of the old man's room, the decay, the grey face with the stubbled hollows matching the colour of the sheets. . . .

All the same, this long-drawn-out agony (as the newspapers might describe it) wasn't fair to him. It was upsetting. He was being upset and that wasn't included in the bargain which, Waggoner considered, he'd struck with Them, with the law. He'd known, naturally, that things would have to be done Their way. But enough was enough and suffering was not included. Definitely not.

Stern with righteous wrath, Waggoner rose in his place. 'Enough!' he intended to say, 'enough of this old pantomime! They've no right . . . I *told* them already.'

But the judge didn't give Waggoner half a chance to say

anything. He raised his hand, for a moment concealing his face: wizened, wrinkled, unnaturally small, for some reason reminding Waggoner of a mosquito—and made extra ridiculous by its framework of long, grubby sheep-curls.

'The prisoner must be silent! He must be seated!'

Waggoner shrugged, hesitated, pondered disobedience for a split-second. One of the warders, the potbellied, morose Mr. Parsons, gave him a sharp and quite unfriendly tap on the shoulder, at the same time almost pushing him down again on his chair.

So he had no alternative. He'd wanted to save time and money, wanted to agree with everything. But they seemed determined to continue, like with a play, a charade. . . . Their lookout, then.

Waggoner fixed his gaze on the window. There was nothing much to be seen through the faint glaze of dust but, outlined against a cloudy, neutral sky, an enigmatic and somehow alien chimney. It was quite an ordinary one—that was the point—and, though Waggoner could only see the top part of it from his place, it gave the impression of belonging to a house, an ordinary house such as might even still be burning homey, dirty, forbidden coal. Of course there was no smoke coming out of it now, but you had the feeling that it might at any moment, and that below there would be an ordinary fire in an ordinary grate, with nice flames licking away at the sooty fire bricks, perhaps with a cat stretching itself in the warmth on a rug, and a woman, feeling the cosy warmth on her legs wondering if the fire was hot enough to toast crumpets. . . .

Waggoner let his thoughts drift thus pleasantly and aimlessly. He didn't want to pay any attention to what was going on, to worry himself for nothing. In due course someone would tell him to get up, and show him where to go. He wouldn't have to speak any more.

'I won't call you to give evidence,' Mr. Fifterley had told him. 'You don't have to. . . . Better not.'

Waggoner was pleased at that, really. He'd never fancied himself as a talker and there was nothing now he wanted to say. Except, of course, what Fifterley had forbidden him to say and for which, apparently, it was too late anyway.

The biggest lie Mr. Fifterley was telling (though in court lawyers' lies were called 'pleading,' Waggoner had learned), was to say that Waggoner hadn't meant to do what he'd done.

It was true, would have been true, to say that he'd only been consciously planning it for a few hours; yet the seeds of the intent must have been there, germinating in his head, for days; perhaps much longer, without his being aware of it himself.

> The needs,
> The seeds of the deeds
> Grew like weeds,

Waggoner rhymed. The habit, which he rather regretted, had been growing on him lately. Stress and strain, he supposed. After all, he'd been under stress and strain for a long time.

He wasn't quite sure at what point, what place in his story he'd have begun, if they'd let him tell it in his own way, straight-forwardly.

He would have to say that Agnes' death had been the real beginning. Because it was only after that that everything had started to go downhill. But really it had all started when the changes had begun, a couple of years before that, even. The changes that preceded and in a way foreshadowed Agnes' death and all that stemmed from it. That must have been the moment (if there had to be one particular one) when the seeds of the deeds had dropped—or rather floated, for they were lighter than thistledown, invisible and impalpable—down to earth, down to Waggoner's portion of earth.

He could, even now, pinpoint the day. It must have been a Thursday, though he couldn't remember the date. Winter; it must have been winter, because in the churchyard they had stood with mud squelching from their boot-soles and wind scouring their faces with sleet.

It was a Thursday, because Agnes always made kippers for his tea on Thursdays. Waggoner, who liked the smell of them, had gone straight through into the kitchen, wondering why she hadn't called out to him as she always did: 'Is that you, dear?'

To which Waggoner always answered: 'Yes.'

He would have come along the street, probably hurrying, because if it was winter it would have been cold, already dark, and he would have been anxious to get indoors. He knew he wouldn't catch the news on telly, but there was always the same later— not that he was interested, really. Occasionally there was some item in the following chitchat that did interest him; but mildly, and not often. Still, he liked to have it turned on. The voices and sounds made a mind-cushioning background to the meal.

Sometimes the voices were suave, phoney-homey, of the telly-people themselves: a breed begotten by electronics and born of the tube. Or they would be the halting utterances of those Waggoner considered 'real people,' like himself.

He preferred them, though they were usually plaintive or aggressive, airing grumble or grievance. When he bothered to listen, he usually agreed with what they said, or were trying to say. They would be objecting to fare rises or rent rises, to having their children driven a long way to school, or to having traffic and other peoples' children routed past their doors.

He and Agnes had never had children—for reasons which Waggoner had never bothered about, since he was just as glad— so really there was a whole area of such grievances which was a closed book to them both. He and Agnes couldn't feel very strongly about free school milk and meals, one way or the other.

Fares, now; that was different. Waggoner paid goodness knows how many times as much to get to the office as when he'd started work at Elmwood, Braine & Hostace. Of course, that was thirty years ago, admitted; and Waggoner's wages, bad as they were compared with most, had gone up a few times too.

But Waggoner thought it was right for people to grumble, if they had reason or not. It changed nothing, everyone knew; but Waggoner believed that They didn't want to upset too much the ordinary people who spoke their grumbles into the telly-cameras' chilly eyes, holding their heads stiffly as though invisible iron stalks supported their necks at odd angles. They spoke through gapped teeth, often incoherently, and it was often impossible to make out what they said. But it must be a good thing, Waggoner was sure, and vicariously enjoyed their indignation and outrage.

Anyway, that Thursday, then, as it must have been, Waggoner

had eased his feet from his shoes into the slippers waiting in the hall, sniffing in the salty-sweet kipper-smell.

'Agnes?' Perhaps the sizzling of the fish, which was quite loud, had prevented her from hearing him come in. 'Agnes?'

'Yes.' She had heard, after all. She came to the door of the kitchen, the dark doorway under the stair well. Her pinafore was clean and crisp, as always—she owned three and changed every day.

Waggoner was puzzled. 'Kippers,' he said. 'Thursday. Good!'

But he already knew that, kippers or not, Thursday or not, everything was not well. Agnes held a telegram; the orange envelope, the ugly buff-coloured message meant trouble, though he couldn't think . . . but disruption, in any case.

'It's Mother,' Agnes said. She was never much of a talker, and her voice even had a rusty sound, creaking as though from disuse. She put the telegram in his hands, but it was crumpled and he didn't want to read it. He had a curious reluctance to see the words, to see their actual physical shape, black letters on the buff-brown paper. He must have known, somehow, already then, so soon, that this was the first breech in the bastion of use and comfortable custom.

'She's gone! Betty says. . . . It was last night, must have been.' Agnes didn't seem upset so much as put out. She hadn't seen her mother more than a few times since they'd been married; not so much from enmity or dislike as from sheer indifference in the face of distance.

The mother still lived—had still lived—in the small Lancashire town where Agnes had been born. The other sister, Betty, had shared a house, made into two flats, with the mother and father.

Agnes' father was a sailor, a merchant-seaman and he still worked, though he must have been getting on, Waggoner reckoned. He followed Agnes into the kitchen. He saw that she had put up her hair in curlers, which she only did as a prelude to going somewhere special. Apparently she felt it her duty to go up to Newtown.

The table was laid as usual, the loaf on its board, teapot in its cosy. Agnes would tell him everything in due course. The telly was ready on its wheeled stand. Waggoner switched it on in passing, the action automatic.

'What was it with her, then?' Waggoner asked, not to seem uncaring.

'The usual.' Agnes turned up the gas under the kippers and started cutting bread. The mother had suffered from a heart condition for some years and had had a number of attacks. This, apparently had been another, but fatal.

The telly had warmed up. The screen showed an interesting abstract design of lines, wildly fluctuating then settling into the familiar picture of the commentator, talking, talking, with great seriousness, impressively, you could tell that, though Waggoner hadn't turned up the sound—not quite timely yet, fastidiously. Turning on entertainment before some discussion at least might seem callous; though he knew that, in fact, there was nothing useful to say.

'You'll be going up? To the funeral?' He already knew she would.

'Yes.'

'When will it be? She say?'

' "Writing," the telegram says. So she'll let me know. . . . Next week, I s'pose.' Agnes paused in the act of forking the kippers from pan to plates. 'You coming?'

Waggoner turned the thought over in his mind. 'Yes,' he said. 'Yes. Well, I s'pose . . . ?'

'Yes,' Agnes confirmed that he ought to go with her.

'All right.'

Waggoner considered it a waste of money to buy an evening paper, getting all the news he wanted, and more, really, on the telly. But he usually picked one up which had been left on the train by some less provident person: it was one of the small mysteries of life to Waggoner that people, and quite a lot of them at that, should buy papers and then, without the slightest chance of having had their money's worth, should then abandon them. Still, one man's meat, as they said. . . . This evening he had a paper with a gruesome headline about some sex murder and he wouldn't have minded looking at that over his supper. But as a further gesture

15

of respect for Agnes' putative grief he'd left the paper outside in his overcoat pocket.

It was true that Agnes wasn't showing any grief; but that was her way. A mother was a mother, after all. You only had one. . . . Waggoner, with a fleeting memory of his own, thought it was just as well, perhaps. Fathers, too. . . . 'Andy?' he asked. 'What about Andy?'

'Dad? What about him?'

'He home? He know?'

'Oh!' Agnes stopped eating. The idea was a new one. 'Must do,' she decided at last. 'Betty will have notified them, the Line. They'll let him know. His wife, after all.'

'They couldn't not let a man know about his wife,' Waggoner agreed. 'But what about the funeral? How'll they get him home? He far?'

Agnes shrugged that she didn't know.

'They'd better,' Waggoner said ominously. 'They couldn't not get him home for the funeral. Fly him back, they'd have to, if necessary.'

'Yes.'

'Betty didn't say when it'll be?'

'Well, "writing" . . . that'd be it, then.'

'Because,' Waggoner said in the special, slightly plummy voice he used for anything connected with the office, 'I'll have to warn them. At work. Tell them when I'll be away.'

'Yes. There'll be time.' Agnes also had a special way of speaking of this important subject, aspirating more carefully than usual and with rounder vowels. Waggoner was, when all was said and done, a white-collar worker and even though he wasn't very high in the hierarchy and was far worse paid than, for instance, Betty's husband, Tom, who was a bricklayer, yet it still counted for something. Most of the neighbours were also their inferiors in this respect.

Agnes went over to the telly and turned up the sound. As usual at this particular time, there was loud discord, while the screen flashed bewildering lights. It was the time when they had Pop; neither Waggoner nor Agnes liked this very much, but as all the channels did it simultaneously there was no escape.

Although the assailment was particularly unpleasant tonight, Waggoner was pleased that Agnes, by her action, had returned them to normalcy, at least for the evening.

He hadn't known, then, how short-lived, impermanent, and unattainable normalcy was to be.

CHAPTER 3

Agnes was a good girl, a good wife. One could say (correction: one *could* have said) that she had been a perfect wife, and he'd always thought so. It wasn't appreciating her when it was too late, as most did. Of course, there had been that niggling annoyance about the slippers and even that wasn't her fault alone. Waggoner would only have had to say the word. . . .

She had of her own accord started the habit of leaving his slippers for him three steps inside the front door, at the bottom of the stairs, so that he could put them on immediately on entering the house. It was meant entirely for his convenience, Waggoner knew, and not from any finnicky house-proudness, or from laziness to save cleaning rugs and lino. No; Agnes was as clean as anyone about the house but she didn't carry it to excess and she didn't chivvy Waggoner about neatness and such. She simply cleared up after him, which was probably easier for her.

She must have seen that his first action when arriving home was to take off his shoes. Waggoner's feet hurt him by evening; always had. He had 'difficult' feet; even shoe salesmen always remarked it. No ordinary shoe size or fitting was made to suit him. Either they pinched—exacerbating his corns and torturing his bunions— or they were too loose, which caused burning and blisters.

There must have been a first occasion when the slippers were there waiting for him. Everything has a beginning of some sort, even the world itself, though people may be divided as to the where, when, and how of it. But Waggoner couldn't remember the first time the slippers had been there, so insiduously had the habit insinuated itself into the fabric of his life.

Unfortunately Agnes hadn't the power of visualizing that which she had not seen—which is called imagination—and Waggoner knew she couldn't be blamed for that. So what she had not realised was that Waggoner, entering, had to walk *towards* the slippers; and that therefore the toes, rather than the heels, should have been similarly aligned. Undeniably, a pair of slippers facing towards you have a generally welcoming and hospitable appearance: rather like a dog with wagging tail. But the sad fact was that every single day of Waggoner's working life he was obliged to walk around the slippers—an extra additional three steps just when least bearable— before he could ease his aching feet. How many painful miles did that amount to in a lifetime?

Waggoner was aware that this was a petty thing. He could, for instance, simply bend down and turn the slippers round. But he felt that that would be slightly ridiculous, slightly undignified— rather like serving oneself breakfast in bed: feasible and possible but fatuous.

He could have spoken to Agnes about it ('By the way, please point my slippers the other way round'). After years had passed she would be surprised, and with reason, so that seemed a bit silly, too. So he had accepted the minor inconvenience together with the major bliss of their being there at all. This juxtaposition, this dichotomy, Waggoner supposed was life, like his own inability to speak the first time, so that the habit had become fixed, a fixture like the snapshot of a familiar face caught forever in a quirky grimace.

Later, in the long, long afterwards, Waggoner was to call all that period the Time of the Slippers. He'd heard (no doubt it would have been on telly), that the Chinese named their years: there would be the Year of the Toad, for example, or the Year of the Tiger.

Well, on the whole they had been good years, the Years of the Slippers—looking back on them—when the slippers had been wait- ing there each evening, in the right place but the wrong position.

There must, he supposed now, have been many pairs in all that time; but Agnes would have changed each pair as they became shabby and shredded for another, identical but new. Waggoner had never noticed the changeover.

With exquisite relief, having stretched and massaged his tingling toes and ensconced them in the slippers, he would exchange the entry-greeting with Agnes, take the evening paper from his pocket, if he'd managed to nab one, and enter the kitchen. The evening took over from the day.

Agnes would then say: 'Ready in a minute,' or 'Shan't be long.' The latter would signify a wait of up to five minutes, and was usual when the meal consisted of sausages or eggs, which Agnes cooked only when he was already there.

Waggoner would grunt acknowledgement as he sank on to his chair: the words from her and the sound from him almost speaking themselves: semaphore, regaining-the-cave sound, registration of arrival at home port—all those things.

His chair was a padded one, for they used the kitchen for their evening telly to save heating the front room. There would be a clean plastic cloth on the table, a bottle of tomato sauce and a jar of pickles. The tea-cosy on the brown earthenware pot had been knitted by Agnes' mother. She gave them one every Christmas (one year the stripes were yellow and mauve, the next blue and pink); and then Agnes gave away the old one to a local charity.

Agnes and he didn't usually have much to say to each other: they scarcely ever spoke of anything other than the immediate and the concrete. Rarely Agnes would recount some detail about their neighbours, but as she was neither curious nor companionable, unless something came her way she wouldn't go looking, as she put it herself.

It was not, in any case, a street nor a neighbourhood for dramas, neither good enough to attract thieves nor mean enough for vandals. The small houses clung together in pairs, like Siamese twins, faced with dingy brick and roofed in slate the colour of drowned men's lips. Each roof-top bore a spike which Waggoner had supposed to be a lightning-conductor until he saw a film of German soldiers in World War I, with the Kaiser's guards all wearing exactly the same ones on their helmets. As he had never heard of people wearing lightning-conductors (though, come to think of it, why not?) Waggoner concluded that they must be for decoration, ugly as they were.

Each house was enclosed about with a hedge, usually of privet, dust-green or mustard-yellow, and some had a rosebush or two sandwiched between hedge and front-room window; on these, in summer, the roses would riot in quite disproportionate profusion. The windows were nearly all discreetly shrouded with net curtains.

Although their street was quite straight (if uphill), it was called Pontefract Crescent. The neighbourhood had been built up in late Victorian times; the street names all resounded with the glories of empire, of border, battle, and castle, conquests and colonies, when all those had been considered worthy of celebration. The names breathed gun smoke, sounded like the tucket of trumpets, the roll of drums.

The houses had been meant for middle-sized families of small tradesmen; but these had long gone, either to the Elysian Fields or on to council estates. Clerks and salesmen on commission lived there now, and not-very-new cars dotted the curbs. Most had been there a long time and therefore enjoyed controlled rents, as did the Waggoners. Most had improved the houses by adding bathrooms; the Waggoners' house had already had one, which was just as well, for Waggoner didn't believe in spending money on other peoples' houses!

Sometimes, until they turned up the sound on the telly, waiting for something they could listen to without needing to work their brains, Agnes might ask Waggoner what sort of day he'd had. He would have to think before answering, for one day was very like another.

Today? Today? What had happened? The new office boy, Ron, had broken his stapler. . . . But no; that was last week and he'd told Agnes about it already. Mr. Hostace . . . he'd called the typist, Amanda, into his office, and he'd given her a telling off. Waggoner hadn't known what it was for and hadn't troubled to ask—wasn't interested enough. But they knew it was a talking-to, because you could hear Mr. Hostace's voice raised in the squeal of protest denoting his ire. Amanda might probably be leaving them, he supposed, by next week. But another would take her place, and it would be impossible to tell one from the other, so far as he was concerned. . . .

'Miss Hirsh,' he'd dredge up at last. 'Miss Hirsh is away again, with one of her colds I suppose. Always something.'

'More work on your shoulders,' Agnes would say, with in-

22

dignation on his behalf, with sympathy. Waggoner would shrug: a slow, weary gesture. But as a matter of fact it didn't affect him or his work if Miss Hirsh was there or not. She was Mr. Hostace's secretary, and he didn't seem to care if he waited for his letters or for his ledger to be made up, or whatever it was Miss Hirsh did for him. Kept himself busy with his crossword puzzles instead; quite happily, too, Waggoner supposed.

Agnes, who had never met Miss Hirsh, had nonetheless built up an enmity for her. 'Her colds! Nothing else to do with herself, that's what it is. Old maid!' she said now.

'I don't know,' Waggoner temporized. He had no feelings about Miss Hirsh one way or the other. If he were to hear that she had suddenly dropped dead, or even see it happen, he would certainly be quite unmoved and his only consideration would be how he himself would be affected. He had never thought about her as a person; to him she was just another piece of office furniture together with his own battered wooden desk, the chipped green filing cabinets, and the drugget on the floor between the desks.

Over the years Miss Hirsh's bush of dusty hair had become grizzled, her long face yellower. Unchanged, though, from when she had first come to work at Elmwood, Braine & Hostace, at about the same time as Waggoner, was her style of dress. She still wore a V of lace in the neck of her jumpers: an item of clothing which had then been called a 'modesty' and had disappeared from women's wardrobes as from the language, surviving only with her. She wore strapped shoes of almost antique design, and stockings of thick-woven cotton. She emitted a faint effluvium of lavender-water and moth balls, which was not unpleasant, and wore a fob watch dangling from a brooch shaped like a lover's knot.

After some desultory conversation of this kind, Agnes would wash up, while Waggoner, having turned the telly sound full on, settled himself for the evening's listening.

Fortunately neither of them had very pronounced preferences or dislikes, accepting what was shown with reactions ranging from mild interest to resignation. They quite liked programmes figuring people they found similar to themselves, whether in interviews or 'series.' Ordinary plays they usually thought silly, dealing with situations not common in real life; for the same reason they were bored by documentary and news programmes which dealt with riots and rebellions, wars and earthquakes, famines and invasions, airplane crashes and politicians.

The only exception to this had been the flights and landings of the astronauts. One would expect that, since it all happened quite literally out of this world, Waggoner would not have had the slightest interest; it was surprising to him, himself, to find that he was strangely stirred.

Watching the grotesque white figures, which looked like the advertisements they used to have for tyres, ponderous placing of elephantine paces on the moon's surface, Waggoner felt a great surge of longing, a sense of almost physical deprivation. That, there, was the future, glimpsed as though through a rent in the veil covering its mysteries. It was remote from him not alone in space but also in time, belonging, he felt, as much to the future as historical reconstructions did to the past. It was the future happening now: a future in which Waggoner would have no part, no place. Waggoner would never pace that arid surface (not, of course, that he wished to do so); he would never, could never, be there. Inasmuch as that place, those activities existed, Waggoner was already dead, might never have been born. When men walked the moon as freely as they now did Brighton or Southend beaches, Waggoner would in actual fact be under the earth of this planet, never having reached the other. . . .

So Waggoner was repelled as well as fascinated, at least for a time, though when moon travel became something of a cliché he tended to avoid programmes heralded by the great priapic rockets soaring skywards. Why make yourself miserable with morbid thoughts, after all? And there was always something else to turn to. So by the time they'd had their nighttime milk drink ('a food of the night,' or 'gives you a *good* day tomorrow') the evenings of the Years of the Slippers had blended, or rather faded into all the other evenings, as alike as the days had been, and as unremarkable.

So Waggoner's evening rituals were mostly pleasant. The morning ones yielded fewer satisfactions and more aggravations.

His chief cause for complaint was that the 8:17 train arrived in London five minutes earlier than he needed for getting to his office on time, even if the weather was good enough for dawdling. But the next one, leaving at 8:35, would have got him there seven minutes late, which of course was as unthinkable as being too early.

Hating waste as he did, Waggoner really resented the daily lost five minutes, which, added together, totalled hours, days: a slice of his life spent staring into the windows of the few shops on his way—an office stationer's, a few newspaper shops, a barber's, and the enigmatic façades of a number of banks.

Sometimes it happened that Waggoner's train did get in late, due to some dislocation of the service caused by weather, fog, snow, ice on the rails, or excessive rain, all of which were a source of perpetual surprise and unpreparedness to British Rail. This lateness, which was not his fault, Waggoner considered an additional, gratuitous affront. It was never sufficient to be a real abridgement of his working hours, and was scarcely remarked, though he might have to hurry himself a little to catch up. So he was doubly deprived, both by punctuality and tardiness.

What was extraordinary (among so much that was wonderful and inexplicable in the ordering of the universe), was the fact that in all these years that Waggoner had been using the line, the only thing remaining unchanged was the train-times from his station to the city. The very stations were changed beyond recognition—now looking more like conveyor belts rather than the dingy cathedrals of yore; the numbers of people travelling had multiplied and conceivably more trains ran. But not for Waggoner. Inexorably there remained the 8:17 and the 8:35, with nothing between the two. Empires rose and fell, monarchies expired, and republics bloomed and faded, science discovered new hells and promised new heavens and the day was about to dawn when people could be born, live, and die like battery hens, in neat compartments, and never have to use trains at all. But in the meantime Waggoner suffered his daily affront.

It was really a wonder that they never came and made interviews for the telly among the passengers. If they had, he was sure everyone would say that 8:20, if not 8:22, would be far better for all concerned. But did they come asking such questions on his train, at his station? They did not!

The reason, though, was clear. Those people, the smart, with-it young men and the trim, trendy yet obviously bright girls whom you saw doing the interviewing (thrusting little mikes like woolly-gloved baby-fists into peoples' faces), were not about to get out of their comfortable beds at that sort of hour in the morning. . . .

So Waggoner knew, really, that it would never happen to him, but he had dispersed the tedium of many a homeward journey in mental colloquy with a telly-man or -girl. In the mornings he was generally still numb from sleep and didn't bother with public pronouncements, even imaginary ones. But of course, if they ever came he would be ready, with all the rehearsing he'd done. He'd tell them, all right!

('Tell us, Mr. . . . ?'

'Waggoner. . . . John Waggoner.'

'Ah, yes. Mr. Waggoner. What do you think of the service on this line? Are the trains punctual? Clean? What improvements would you suggest?')

That would be his cue to launch out. Quite a tirade it would be before he finished. He would be eloquent, loquacious. . . . He knew, naturally, that nothing would be changed by anything he said.

Still, They ought to be told, sometimes, and there was always the chance that They might not have realised. . . . After all, for the most part They were beneficent: everything was kept running, drains, gas, street-lights, telephones, things like that. Yes, and trains, too, however little peoples' convenience was taken into account.

It seemed, sometimes, as though They were purposely keeping things difficult for the ordinary man, for Waggoner. Perhaps They didn't want people to get soft, as they would if everything was easy, perfect . . . like pets in padded cages they'd be.

Waggoner had never decided whether They cared, whether They were even aware of his existence, except as cards in computers where all the facts were stored and the accounts, of taxes and such, were made up.

If They really did take care of things in that sort of way, then it was just as well that Waggoner hadn't been allowed to get soft. He'd had to fend for himself; had needed strength as well as cunning. And, particularly, he'd needed patience and endurance.

In these he had been trained by all those trains! As his first day in court came to an end Waggoner was absorbed by this thought. The aphorism was so neat that he was tempted to accept it for that reason alone. But he knew, of course, that, apposite though it might be, it was only partly true.

He had come through, survived, because he had seen through Their system, found out how it worked, and beaten it at its own game.

Now that all his troubles and hardships were over there was a pleasant sense, a feeling akin to victory, in looking back on it all. He was like a climber on the peak of a mountain, looking down at the long weary track he'd hauled himself up. Made being where he was all the more worth while.

CHAPTER 4

As soon as he'd accepted the fact that he was going only to be a cipher, and a silent cipher at that, Waggoner had not only allowed his attention to wander from what went on in the court, but deliberately divorced himself from it. The proceedings had nothing to do with the real, the essential Waggoner, who could set off on byways of speculation and memory that were quite engrossing.

In fact he wouldn't even have been quite certain that this was the second day but for definite recollections of the intervening evening and night.

These had been interesting. A new warder—new to Waggoner, at least—had fetched in his supper. On enquiry he had learned that the familiar Mr. Parsons (bad-humoured, as plump people so often are, contrary to popular myth and Shakespearian axiom), was now on another 'tour of duty,' which probably meant he was having a day's leave. Mr. Harris was never on in the evenings. The replacement, who gave his name as Mr. Clambers, had simply put down the tray of food in front of Waggoner without asking what he wanted, or at least preferred.

The meal had consisted of several slices of meat, similar to, but not beef, mashed potato, bread and butter, and a slice of cake with a cup of cocoa. And, although he had previously been vexed at having to chose his own menu, Waggoner was now just as peeved at having his acceptance of this meal taken for granted. The truth was that he enjoyed it, though the cake did have the inevitable institutional flavour of cardboard and the cocoa the prison smell —to which he was already getting used—of chlorine.

What continued to impress Waggoner afresh at every mealtime was the china, which was very white, gleaming, and tremendously heavy. It was unlike any Waggoner had ever seen before, and he assumed that it must be specially made for Her Majesty's Prisons. All the same, he hardly expected that such good stuff would be used in the regular jails, for condemned, ordinary prisoners. There, surely, they would be given metal plates and cups (or perhaps, nowadays, it might be plastic instead); and this seemed to him quite suitable. He was sure he would get used very quickly to tin or enamel plates; as for plastic ones, he was quite used to them already, from home.

Although Waggoner was determined that the court and all its appurtenances and persons would not affect him except as entertainment, he was not averse to distractions from the outside world.

Nature, surprisingly enough, had entrée of a limited sort there. There was, for instance, a shaft of sunlight, which, having first penetrated the layers of atmosphere surrounding the earth (Waggoner pictured this as a kind of globular sandwich), then had to pierce the filmy clouds, and then the hazed miasma of massed breath—the exudations and exhalations of billions of humans and their dwellings and all their works, all the steaming dung-heaps of human enterprise. Having miraculously evaded the roofs and chimneys and spires of buildings, then the structure of the court building itself—which was unusually complex—the ledges and cornices surrounding its battlements and windows, the grime and mist on the glass itself, the light ray shone, actually showed a beam, straight into the room. It made a strangely drab splotch on the floor, and subfusc patterns on human hides and hair, on furniture and papers and books and clothing. Its angle was of necessity acute and Waggoner could be practically certain that it would never move enough to reach his place, his chair, his person. Which, when he considered it, was just as well; he had no desire for celestial limelight. The human sort was quite enough!

There were also sounds filtering in, though these were less remarkable, being, by their very nature, the product of mere human busyness and purposefulness. There was the roar and howling of jet planes, occasionally so loud that people had to stand, mouths held idiotically agape like verbal piggy-banks, to wait their passing. The traffic noise was a constant, subliminal, and not unpleasant hum, though orchestrated with an occasional screech of hastily applied brakes or angry hooter.

From within the building itself, when the door of the court was opened, could be heard the hollow clang of feet, the click of heels on stone floors, voices of ushers calling (as they had summoned him, who was already there), even stray snatches of conversation, suddenly silenced. And, close by, of course, a multiplicity of sounds: the speaking, rustling of movement and stirring of limbs, of clothing and chairs, books, files . . .

Everything that happened inside the court, the spoken words, the phrases and sentences they formed, the very presence of these people, would not have been but for himself, but for Waggoner. . . . He was the prime cause; he heard but need not listen unless he wished.

There had been a time, not very long before, when this happy state of affairs had not existed. Waggoner had not, then, been the arbiter of what was or was not. Then—before he had taken his own fate into his own hands, rendering it and himself to Them, he had been only a victim of his own needs, which had become un-manageable. His body's discards had made a desert around him, a wasteland littered with dirty socks, bottles curdled with dregs of milk, half empty tins of food, all green-moulded. The mounds of refuse and waste were not high enough to conceal him, the dust-smelling curtains of his house hid but could not contain him. To be there, stranded among it all, caused him agoraphobia.

He had felt denuded and yet menaced by the treachery of his own being; and this, being unescapable, was very frightening. How was it possible to escape from his own needing self, which filled every cranny and crevice of existence?

Waggoner gave one of his rare smiles. He had found the way. He had conquered and come through.

So that Thursday evening, when he'd opened the door and gone into his house, there had been nothing special at all for Waggoner to anticipate, beyond the immediate prospect of kippers for tea and later the perennial series that Agnes and he both ac-corded a degree more than their usual toleration.

If he had wanted to look ahead into the future, he could see himself retiring in a few years. Which would mean less money, of course (quite a bit less, since Elmwood, Braine & Hostace hadn't organized any pension fund); but Waggoner had heard that older people didn't need so much, and anyway he was sure they could live more cheaply if they had to. He wouldn't need the daily clean shirt, for instance, nor the lunch in a restaurant which he now had with his luncheon vouchers. Agnes would make him something at home and he supposed they'd both eat less, being older. There wouldn't be any fares to pay; yes, there would be economies, some welcome, some not. But they'd manage.

After the first apprehension, the shock of the telegram and all that, Waggoner had decided that the death of Agnes' mother wouldn't alter anything; and it was clear that Agnes thought the same. The old lady wouldn't have had anything of value to leave and what she had would go to Andy, her husband.

Of course there was this funeral to upset the pattern. But it was no more than a nuisance, after all, and a break in routine wasn't entirely unwelcome. They wouldn't mind, at the office, him taking the time off. He wasn't one to take every chance to stay away from work; in fact he hardly ever did. And the funeral of a mother-in-law, after all. . . . So that would be all right.

Waggoner remembered (because it was another small but significant break in the regular pattern) that that night, after the telegram, he hadn't dropped off to sleep as quickly as usual.

He'd tossed and turned quite a bit; he couldn't have said exactly why, or what it was all about. And when Agnes mumbled sleepily, asking what was the matter and was he ill or something, he couldn't even have told her, even if he'd wanted, even if she'd woken up enough to listen.

Because he didn't believe in such things as premonitions; although, if there is still anything remaining in the human being of its animal origins, this primeval, this almost amoebal sensing of future dangers might well be the last trait to disappear. And perhaps, then, this atavistic tingling and unrest was his blood trying to tell him that life (or what was life to Waggoner) was being threatened from afar. And that the first signs of that which would eventually destroy his lair, his hidey-hole, his water hole, his food trail, had appeared. Ancient neurons flashed along nerve trails like trackers in the jungle . . . nerve trails which were confused and uncredited, coarsened with cardboard railway tickets, nickel coins, stainless steel cutlery, and plastic toothbrushes.

The whisper was that he should beware, take action: not sleep, but move, run, hide. But of course Waggoner didn't understand the message, not even the language in which it spoke; and wouldn't have known what to do about it if he had.

In fact it was already too late, for external forces, external pressures, were Waggoner's imperative now; but since his atavistic antennae didn't know this they continued to throb and generally kept him awake, so that he began to worry that if he didn't get enough sleep he'd be tired the next day; and this made him more restless.

Then he began to think about the journey to and from Newtown. He hoped it wouldn't be too tiring; he hoped they'd be able to manage only to stop the one night; he hoped nothing would be expected of them. He hoped . . . he hoped . . .

In the event everything was exactly as predictable, knowing Betty and Tom Harkness, Agnes' sister and her husband, knowing Andy Matthews, her father, knowing Newtown and especially knowing their way of life and living which, after all, were very like their own. The exception to this was Andy, who was more or less a visitor in his own home, from being away most of the time, and he didn't alter anything. Waggoner had hardly ever seen him before and didn't take much notice now. He'd seemed a quiet, harmless old man.

The Waggoners had to rise at dawn to catch the early train which would get them to Newtown by mid-day, in time for the funeral. There all was dismal, grey, and rain-sodden as it always seemed to be: impossible to imagine the town in any other mood. It would scowl at summer, surely, with sultry oppressiveness and thunderstorms; the gold of autumn and the green of spring would anyway have no showing among its concrete, stone, and brick.

While they stood around the muddy grave hole (heads lowered respectfully so that icy raindrops crept down their necks), Waggoner thought that there ought to be specially appointed towns for the death industry: towns which by character and mood were suited to it and where the population could take easily to the disposing of the dead.

There might, to carry the idea further, be other places suitable for birth, sunny, seaside, lighthearted places with parks and pleasure palaces and piers lined with slot machines. As for living . . .

Waggoner had pondered that, standing there, not listening to the funeral service (any more than he now did to the trial). But he didn't know the answer now any more than he had then. He couldn't really picture any ideal place or way to live, so he had opted, hadn't he, for prison? The best available.

On the other side of the grave, opposite him, was Betty, an uninspiring sight with her round, meaty face centred with a red blob of nose, its nostrils upturned to the grizzling sky. One could not tell if she was moved by her mother's death; impossible even to guess what feelings, if any, stirred beneath that sturdy, navygabardined exterior. A black band encircled her sleeve (but Waggoner had one of those, too, provided before leaving the house of bereavement); perhaps it signified something.

Andrew Matthews, the newly made widower, the sailor returned from the sea, looked bewildered rather than sad. It was rain, not tears, that glistened on his seamed face; his badger-streaky hair was wet, too, spiked around his bared head. He kept looking round, as though wondering what he was doing there, land, or rather mud all about him instead of water and the body of his wife (however little regarded) being lowered into that dark, slimy hole.

Of course, They had got him home in time. He had explained to Waggoner, while they waited together for the hired car to take them to the churchyard, that he was only on coastal routes nowadays, working on freighters. They were little more than seagoing barges, he said, plying between one English port and another. Waggoner, who had thought a sailor's life meant white sails and blue tropic seas, was aware of disappointment.

But the old man had missed the days of sailing ships; they had been uneconomic by the time he went 'before the mast,' which was already a misnomer. His were the days when ships used steam and coal; the smell of old railway stations had mingled with the salt of his seafaring. The holds and galleys and bunk-rooms of freighters had contained him; the glamour of the far-off lands had not penetrated the rusted sides of those stubby ships nor, ashore, survived the first confrontation with sore-crusted beggars and pimps with their haggard wares. Foreign climes had meant these things to him: the lassitude of heat, the pinch of cold and undecipherable lettering on harbour walls, sour wine or flavoured firewater, the cheating sleight of hand of barmen in sleazy dens. His contact with strange peoples had been with their professional petty parasites trying to weasel out the extra mark or piastre or krone from the sailor starved of land and love; in the waterside alleys the snatch of unknown tongues, words meant for others, sounding furtive, threatening.

He had always returned to the shelter of the fo'c'sle with its familiar faces and sounds with thankfulness. Landscape had been the eternal sea around the sliding decks, or lapping the stones of some unfriendly dock wall afloat with cigarette packets with strange names.

No; he wouldn't miss much when he left the sea for good, as perhaps he would, now. There would be a small pension and what with the Old Age Pension and all he'd have enough to get by. It did sound rather as though, now that his wife was no longer there, life ashore would be bearable.

Betty's face had become even sourer than usual when she heard this. But still Waggoner hadn't seen how any of it was likely to affect him.

He and Agnes had had to spend the night—in extreme discomfort—on Betty's pull-out pull-down put-u-up bed in the parlour. The next morning, in the train back to London, Agnes had explained.

Andy, she told Waggoner, had never cared much for his younger daughter and now, retiring (or being retired, perhaps, for he was sixty-nine and too old, really, even for the slight rigors of the coastal run), he wouldn't want to stay on in the upstairs flat in the family council house in Newtown. Accustomed to the close company of shipmates he wouldn't like either the isolation or living with Betty.

'What does he want, then?' Waggoner couldn't see that it was his business nor why Agnes, who didn't talk just for gossip's sake, was on about it.

'Wants to come and live with us he does,' she said, pulling off her black imitation pigskin funeral gloves and rolling them in a ball.

'To us?' Waggoner was astonished. It was all so sudden, so unexpected.

Agnes merely nodded, watching him.

'But—it wouldn't be more . . . I mean, where's the company for him with us?'

'He'd find it better. He always got on all right with me. And he'd find. There's old folk round our way for him to get to know.'

'Where'd he sleep, then?'

'The upstairs back room, I thought, p'raps. . . . Besides, he'd pay his way and it might even be worth it,' Agnes said.

'You want it, then?' Waggoner was rather surprised, never having thought about his wife's feelings towards her father, though without supposing any particular fondness. And she still hadn't said that she was keen on the idea, only that it was there, and was possible.

She shrugged in answer. The train was passing through a perfectly flat stretch entirely covered with seemingly identical houses. It was impossible to tell whether they were large or tiny as doll's houses, for there were no human figures to provide a scale of comparison. Agnes stared at this scene as though seeking inspiration.

'It'd be worth it,' was all she found to say again. 'What with what he's got coming in . . . might have saved a bit, for all I know.'

This aspect had not struck Waggoner; if, as well as paying his way, the old man had a bit to leave . . . well, it'd be something to look forward to. But what would it be like, having another person in the house? What would be changed? Certainly there must be some, however slight. And inconveniences: meals, mealtimes put out, not being able, perhaps, to use the bathroom, the lavatory, just when he wanted, without competition from another man.

'He wouldn't be any trouble.' Agnes, as so often, knew what

he was thinking. 'He's been a sailor all his life, remember. He's used to looking after himself.'

This was not exactly the reassurance Waggoner needed. On the contrary; he wasn't worried about Andy but about himself. Still, he understood what Agnes meant. Andy, she was saying, in effect, would tuck himself away in a small, neat compartment, just as he had been used to doing on his ship. Waggoner supposed vaguely that sailors slept in hammocks and kept all their worldly possessions in large wooded boxes lined with zinc (to keep the ants from eating through to them). Well, Andy would be able to keep his sea chest in the small room upstairs which, for that matter, already possessed a miniature cupboard. He could bring his own bed from Newtown.

The upstairs room was at present occupied only by a dressmaker's dummy and a sewing machine, which Agnes used, very rarely, when she made herself a dress. Waggoner himself would not be inconvenienced by the need to find another place for these.

'Needs thinking about,' was all he said though, not wanting to commit himself so early on. It would mean change, no doubt about that; and change should be regarded with caution, at the very least. He had a feeling, too, a subtle sense that the shape of things would be different from then on.

He couldn't give the feeling firmer shape or better definition than that; even in his mind it wasn't clear if it was good or bad. But really, he supposed later, all had been settled and accepted in his own mind from Agnes' first mention. After all it was sensible, and a natural sequel to a death in the family to have some adjustment in the living arrangements of the bereaved. And if it didn't work out—well, there was nothing final; the old man could always go away again. It was as simple as that.

So there had probably never been one actual moment in which the coming of Andy to live with them had been decided. There hadn't been any more discussion between Agnes and himself; or, if there had, it had been so inconsequential that it had left no trace on his memory. Agnes had understood how he felt about the matter and it had been agreed without ever having been disagreed.

Either by the old man's deftness or Agnes' clever management or a combination of both, there wasn't even a demarcation line, a date or time that Waggoner could remember and say: 'That was before Andy came,' or 'That must have been after.' There was no essential change.

Simply, the old man was there, living with them; and it was as though he always had been, their lives having been patterned and shaped from the beginning to make place for him.

CHAPTER 5

Thus Andy had become part and parcel of the texture, the warp and woof of their lives, a feature of them, in much the same way as the slippers had done.

His face, rather like that of a mournful old hound, had its accepted place opposite Waggoner at the family table: the unaltered and unaltering progression of sausages to kippers, poached eggs on toast and beans on toast, and the rest of the diurnal fare masticated and, presumably, digested and processed without the slightest infringement of Waggoner's occupancy or prerogatives.

In the corner of the room was an extra but unobtrusive easy chair, worn yet seemly, upright and sturdy, old yet built to last—rather like Andy himself. It faced telly-wards, of course, yet without obtruding on Waggoner's view. As for the programmes, if the old man would ever have preferred any particular one rather than that which his son-in-law watched, he never voiced his inclination. Perhaps he really had none; but Waggoner thought (when he gave the matter any thought at all), that Andy was anxious to stay in the background and not intrude in his and Agnes' way of life in the slightest. Also, having lived for so many years in such close physical contact with many people, he must have known that it wasn't just the mere occupying of space that impinged on others, but the existence of minority preferences and wishes.

Early on Andy must have seen that Waggoner and he had a different way of looking at things. There was one evening when they were watching one of those programmes (waiting for the entertaining part, which came later) which, newsy and topical, was devoted to people complaining, as often, about their homes.

'Three years,' a man was saying bitterly, staring the telly-camera straight in the eye, giving an air of unreality and uncredibility to what he was saying, 'whole buildin' onny three years old, and look at it!' He indicated a tattered festoon of ceiling paper which dangled down almost to his own telly, which gleamed in the background in startling contrast to the damp-blotched walls. 'And here . . .' He pointed to a splintered window frame. 'Lets in the draught, that does. The kiddies . . . can hear them coughin' all night.'

'Shouldn't be allowed,' Waggoner remarked censoriously.

'They oughtn't to allow it,' the telly-tenant echoed mournfully, broken teeth bared in a painful, incongruous smile.

'Shame!' Waggoner agreed.

'It's a shame,' came antiphonally from the set.

'Argh,' Andy interposed, 'a man . . . three years: why doesn't he get busy? Spend a bit of time, isn't long, to mend something, do some odds and ends himself? 'Tisn't much. Silly, to be like that.'

Waggoner was shocked. Since their house wasn't their own, Waggoner had never done more than affix the occasional nail or screw, at Agnes' request. He was no handyman, anyway, and would have thought it improper to work on other peoples' property. Anything as fundamental as a new handle for the lavatory chain was referred to the 'estate,' who obligingly attended to it sooner or later.

This satisfactory state of affairs Waggoner felt to be due to his own cleverness and perspicacity. After all, he could just as easily have taken Agnes into a furnished room when they married. But she had wanted a house, even though it cost more—only marginally so, at that time, but still more. And he had agreed, hadn't he? Perhaps unspoken between them had been the idea that they might have children. They had acquired furniture, frugally and gradually over the years. So Waggoner was really superior to the snaggle-toothed man, who was even now indicating a horde of his 'kiddies,' uniformly leaking at the nose.

'All those kids; poor kids,' Andy murmured.

'The poor kiddies,' the man was saying. 'Isn't their fault, is it? Living like this?'

They gazed vacantly at him and each other. All were sucking

sweets, perhaps provided by the telly-man, to keep them quiet. The man's wife, it appeared, was in hospital, giving birth to another predestined poor kiddy.

'Yar, They did promise to move us,' the man answered a question. 'Till the repairs was done, like . . .'

Andy had shifted in his chair, impatient, disapproving. 'Gormless,' he opined. 'People: waiting to be moved about, waiting to be put places. It's like they were things!'

Waggoner hadn't answered. In spite of the imaginary debates he carried on, he didn't care for discussion with real people; couldn't be bothered, in fact. Andy was old . . . only ten or so years older than himself, true; but still . . . Also he'd had an unusual life, really, so he wouldn't look at things the same as other people. Didn't know life on shore, either, come to that: a seaman.

Waggoner avoided disagreement by heaving himself out of his chair to switch the telly to another channel. The other would have a parallel subject, true—they always carefully timed them, probably so one wouldn't have advantage over the other, to avoid competition—but both had 'shows' billed to come on very soon anyway.

Yes, here the comics came on, between the swirling curtains they kept from the days of real stages. If the Waggoners' set had been colour TV—which it wasn't, not at that price—the curtains would have been rainbow-hued, glorious, gorgeous, as the old music-hall curtains never had been in real life. But instead there were galaxies of brilliant, flashing lights and bewildering patterns that trellised on and off, all too fast for the eye to follow. One could watch them and it was quite fascinating; the idea was that you shouldn't notice the singing . . .

As far as he remembered the old man had never again offered his opinions in controversy. He, too, like Waggoner, probably preferred peaceful silence. Anyway this also helped to make him easy to live with, get along with.

Waggoner was satisfied with the domestic situation, then. Agnes also seemed content and she hadn't said anything about there being extra work, or minding it if there was any. Andy's contribution to the household budget meant that they could put away a half a pound a week more than before. So everything was all right.

'Guilty, my lord,' Waggoner had intended, had wanted to say, 'guilty as charged.' He had wanted there to be no mistake, no misunderstanding. The last phrase he had heard on the telly, and wasn't quite sure if it was correct, but that was the sense of it anyway.

But he hadn't been allowed to say anything of the sort: quite the opposite in fact, though Mr. Fifterley had explained that everyone would understand; things couldn't be done like that.

At the moment he was in the middle of a peroration—shaped like a question—with which he was trying to make that very nice young policeman contradict himself or sound as if he was. This, Waggoner knew, was called cross-examination, but, he told himself, the only thing cross about it was Fifterley himself. The policeman was only telling the truth; he had been carefully correct and also been kind to Waggoner, as though he were the elder of the two, and he Waggoner's father instead of three decades younger at least.

'This warning,' Mr. Fifterley was saying, in a sarcastic voice (pitched to insinuate that the answer, whatever it might be, was untrue, or irrelevant), 'this warning that you *say* you gave . . .'

'I did give it, sir.'

'If you would kindly not interrupt? I was about to say: this answer which you—*gave*, then, to Mr. Waggoner. Was that before or after he'd made the alleged statement?'

'He made a statement before I could say anything.'

'So you only warned him that his statement might be given in evidence *after* he'd made it?'

The young man thought this over for a moment. 'It was in response to a statement made by him that I was there in the first place.'

'Oh quite, quite. . . . There is no disagreement about the phone call. We are discussing, finding out—*trying* to find out—what was said after you were in the house.'

'He spoke as soon as he opened the door.'

'He spoke as soon as he opened the door,' Mr. Fifterley repeated the sentence weightily. 'You had not warned him then?'

'Not then. I . . .'

And so it went on. Waggoner switched himself off, as it were, willing himself not to hear. It was all too ridiculous; and perhaps, if he'd known there was all this to go through . . . ?

But no; in the end it would all have been worth it, he was sure.

That morning there had been bread and—he supposed—margarine, though 'you couldn't tell the difference,' and porridge; the soup at lunch time was always good, though he'd heard others complain. But then there are some that'll complain about anything.

The stew or occasional steak-and-kidney puddings, the eggs at regular intervals, and especially the pies and spongy jam rolls were all excellent. He called Agnes a good cook, but she'd never been much of a hand with puddings and pies, really.

His wants were modest, Waggoner assured himself, and were amply fulfilled; would be adequately fulfilled, always. . . . He'd heard, even, that those considered elderly or infirm, were given an evening milk drink, and into those categories he considered he might come. It would be quite like home!

Andy had taken after his daughter in not being one to talk much. He'd just join in every now and then with a neutral remark—very much of the kind Agnes and he exchanged—to make it clear that he was present in spirit, as it were, and partaking in the life of the family, though without interfering.

Some evenings the chair in the corner would be empty, but Waggoner didn't take much notice. One evening when there was a political broadcast on the telly (the same on all the channels, so you couldn't escape it, which was a liberty, Waggoner thought, and turned down the sound, just to spite Them), he asked Agnes where the old man had got to.

She had shrugged. 'Cinema, I think.' She was clearly not very interested. 'Where else?'

'By himself?'

'I s'pose so; of course. Who else, then? There is an old peoples' club, but I don't think he liked it there, the once he went. . . . Said all those old people made him feel old.'

43

It seemed strange to Waggoner that anyone should want to turn out at night, into the cold, perhaps, even rain, when there was a chair, warmth, and movement unnecessary and the screen to watch without effort, without extra cost. Still, he supposed the old man had a right to his own eccentricities.

'He get in the way at all during the day? A nuisance?' Waggoner asked, in a rare show of caring, for Andy would naturally be Agnes' burden anyway and it wasn't really his concern. The screen still showed a man with a square white moustache and vaguely military air, talking earnestly. But They hadn't yet found a way of making Waggoner listen and as there was an unnatural hiatus of attention his mind continued to revolve sluggishly (lacking better fodder) round the subject of Andy. 'What's he do all day?'

'Do?' Agnes, unlike Waggoner, was wondering what the man with the white moustache was saying; it must be important to him. Not that she cared, of course. 'Who?'

'Andy . . . your dad. All day . . . what's he do?'

'Oh. Goes out, mostly. Sometimes he'll do the shopping for me, if I tell him what. Sits in the park, mornings, I think. Or the library. Reads the papers there, most like.'

'What park?'

'Where the playground is. Just across the High Street, behind the supermarket. It's just a bit of green, with some benches. The old men sit there, nattering. There's some swings; that's why they call it the playground, meant for the kids but they don't go there.' Agnes did not think it strange that Waggoner, having lived for three decades within half a mile of the open space was unaware of its existence. She herself knew of it because it was behind the shops, which were of the same order of importance in her world as the office was in Waggoner's. 'He reads a lot. He's always been a one for reading,' she said.

Waggoner shook his head in mock disbelief. The things people do! He had seen that the old man brought home heavy tomes, noted that they were usually printed in tiny type on mushy paper: Victorian novels, a dream world which Andy for some reason preferred to that of the telly.

But in the evenings when he sat there, leafing through them, his eyelids drooped and he seemed hardly to be reading them as to be breathing in the musty smell.

'He does his own room,' Agnes said defensively, 'makes his bed, cleans up and such. The bit of shopping saves my legs.' She suffered from varicose veins for as she passed into middle age she had begun to put on weight.

So Andy was a help to her rather than a hindrance. Waggoner was glad. Everything rosy, then. Little changed. There were three mugs of the beverage of the night instead of two . . .

Andy's enjoyment was audible, a sibilant sucking, but nothing disagreeable. Later he would often stand with Agnes at the sink, dishcloth in hand, drying up, humming an unobtrusive, tuneless song.

CHAPTER 6

If there was one thing Waggoner liked it was an organized, orderly, and predictably patterned life, with everything happening just as when he expected, the elements, and parts familiar and the events falling within and shaped to precise limits and boundaries.

It was, after all, from sheer love of order, cleanliness, seemliness, decency, respectability, self-respect, from loyalty to established usages and customs—not to speak of virtues—that he was in this situation today.

Just as there undoubtedly were criminals who would go to any lengths to obtain riches or exotic luxuries, so Waggoner, typical citizen as he considered himself, had been prepared to go to certain well-defined lengths to retain the privileges due to typical citizens. There was, he remembered, something he'd learned in school about a 'village Hampden,' or some such name: a citizen who had become martyred for insisting on his rights. Waggoner was no more or less than a village—or one would have to say a suburban—Hampden. But he was not demanding revolutionary changes, departures from tradition. On the contrary: he deeply desired everything to stay as it had always been.

Therefore he had been quite satisfied with Andy and how he had managed to make himself disappear into the background. At his office, at work, for some time, a period during which he was lulled and disarmed, all continued as usual too. There nothing changed except such constantly changing factors (the changes becoming commonplace thereby), as the identities of the office juniors.

Waggoner had little to do with them directly, so the changes were really only the names: from Mabel, Doris, and Marjorie in the early years, through Marylyn and Lucille and Shirley, to the present succession of Samantha and Amaryllis and Tracey. He had—without excitement—watched skirts rise from calf-length to groin and then descend again. Hair had grown from cropped caps to shingles, risen into elaborate beehives and, lately, dropped in depressing drapes to cover faces which, even without that, he had scarcely time to recognise before their owners were gone. The current incumbent of the post, Sharon, displayed no more than a sharp triangle of nose, which sliced between two sheets of stiff-lacquered hair like a shark fin through water.

Sharon, exactly as had Thomasina and Georgina and Miranda and all her predecessors, at eleven o'clock in the mornings and at four o'clock in the afternoons, made and handed round tea, which, by office custom, was pallid with milk and treacly with sugar. This tea, served in what must, after all these years, be a deliberately random collection of china, with no cup matching any other, nor any saucer, was no different from that which Waggoner had first drunk there thirty-some years before. Of course, a differentiating detail was whether he got the cup with the pink roses, the one with the chipped gilt edge, or one of the earthenware ones: grey and blue, which he rather disliked. The grey one especially was liable to tinge the whole day with its own hue.

Mr. Hostace's tea was always taken in to him in a special, matching cup and saucer with a rather pretty pattern of bunches of violets held together with garlands of gold ribbon. But the tea was the same and when Waggoner had happened to be in there at the time he'd observed that Mr. Hostace helped himself to a ginger biscuit from his own private tin, kept in a drawer of the desk—just as some shady characters did in telly-thrillers—except that they kept whiskey there, which, unlike the ginger biscuits, was illegal, the films being very old.

The older Mr. Hostace had done exactly the same (though the biscuits had been digestives); Mr. Hostace, his nephew, had taken the custom over, as he had everything else, some twenty years before. He was now indistinguishable from his uncle in the memories of his staff, though Waggoner and Miss Hirsh, to mark their own seniority, still called him 'Young Mr. Hostace' between themselves. In reality he must have been about the same age as Waggoner.

Elmwood, Braine & Hostace was one of those concerns which seem to have been founded and to exist only for the purpose of marking time to use up the days of its ageing employes. Once it must have flourished, for it had supported three Victorian households. In some nook or cranny between the harvesting of a few oriental spices and their sale over herbalists' and chemists' counters, the firm's finger (figuratively) was inserted in the process, writing in its minute but cumulative percentage.

The present Mr. Hostace would not have known a galingale from garlic; but then he did not need to know. And he once told Waggoner, in a burst of confidence, quite unprecedented, that he was only keeping the firm going to 'last us out': and that when he himself, Waggoner, and Miss Hirsh would, at more or less the same time, consider themselves due to retire, he would at last, thankfully, close the doors and the books for good.

Since change was intrinsically bad, unless it could be seen to be bearing positive advantages to himself, Waggoner was lucky in that none had really come his way—until, of course, with the beginning, the death of Agnes' mother, when everything that happened show how right he had been to suspect it.

The war had passed Waggoner by. The armed forces had rejected him because of flat feet, a pierced eardrum, and a condition diagnosed as acidosis. None of these had ever bothered him, either before or since, except of course for his feet, which, he knew, were merely unusually shaped. They would have made him unfit for marching, perhaps. But did anybody march in modern wars? And, if they wanted him, could the Army not have had him for the mere cost of specially made boots? Waggoner presumed that they knew they could, but didn't want him even at that price. Which suited Waggoner!

Even the building containing Elmwood, Braine & Hostace remained unscathed but for a few broken windows; at one stage it stood amid the rubble of its neighbours like a solitary, unlovely tooth. The Waggoners' house had also escaped war damage.

Miss Hirsh, the colleague with whom he had most to do, (she

was usually the one who handed him the papers which he filed away and took from him the ones he extracted) had, at some time in the long decades, had her hair cut in a fringe above her scanty eyebrows. But this was scarcely change to concern Waggoner, who really noticed mainly her hands, which, with enlarged, pinkish knuckles, always looked powdery as though with chalk, and reminded Waggoner unpleasantly of a teacher at school whom he had disliked.

Some minor events did leave marks upon whole eras. At some time during the past ten years Mr. Hostace, after more than a generation of buying the office supplies of stationery, had bought—prevailed upon, doubtless, by some smart-aleck salesman —files in a number of colours: red, blue, green, even yellow, in place of the universal buff of the past. This was much resented by Waggoner. Not only were files the tools of his trade, after all; the raw material and framework of his work, and any such fundamental change should not have been made without consultation with him. But he felt that there was some disruption of his life-style. He didn't know whether the choice of colours was arbitrary, accidental, and due only to the smart-aleck's need to turn over stock; or whether the new colours were meant to form the basis of a new system of classification, an idea formed in the lofty executive-decision-making brain of Mr. Hostace during the longueurs of the crossword puzzles.

In any case the whole thing had been psychologically disorientating. Fearful of the answers, he had not asked Mr. Hostace what to do; so he had merely started using the new files, when the old ones were finished, in rotation based on the day of the week when they were begun . . . Monday, for instance, being of course blue.

Remembering this unpleasant dilemma, Wagonner sighed inwardly with relief. He never knew whether he had made the correct decision and appraisal in the matter; never again would he be faced with the need to make such decisions, to cope with such problems.

Miss Hirsh had been bereaved of her mother—only about a year before Agnes—and now lived with and cared for a crippled widowed sister instead. So the daily salutation had to be changed, after nearly a lifetime's use, which also minutely and subtly changed the shape and flavour of the days. Miss Hirsh had been wont to reply to enquiries about her mother's health non-committally, implying that she was as well as could be expected and, if in garrulous mood, simply elaborating this. But she was always ready to expound lengthily about her sister, who, being younger, unfortunate, and with more complicated and incurable illnesses, gave great scope for bulletins.

It had been just after the Christmas when Andy had come to them that, as usual, when the telly started trumpeting about summer holidays, the Waggoners decided on their own: which was always the same and had nothing really in common with the telly ones with their silhouetted nudes, white sandy beaches and faces, glistening with sun-tan oil and beads of sea spray, grinning around tables laden with obviously tax-free foreign drinks, while sumptuous palaces and swimming pools gloated in sunshine.

It had been a day of iron cold. From the leaden sky small particles of ice had fallen. The streets had seemed paved in frozen metal and the people Waggoner passed, hurrying to and from the stations, had not raised their faces from upturned collars. The trains had been filled with unpleasantly smelling steam, clammy as a dead kiss. The house was not very warm, either, but for a small circle round the gas fire.

Andy appeared not to notice the cold but sat in his chair in the corner farthest from the fire; though of course he could have moved nearer if he'd wanted.

Perhaps the telly-ads aroused in him the memory of bygone longings, lusts, and nostalgia for far places and the unknown scene—however unlike he knew the picture and the dream to be from the reality. Whatever the reason, he ventured one of his rare unsolicited remarks.

'What about you?' he had asked—of either or both of them— 'What about you going abroad? For your holiday? Make a change.'

'Abroad? Us?' It was dismissal, not question, from Agnes.

'Cheap enough these days,' the old man observed. The screen was even then blazoning the fact that they could have a 'holiday in the sun' from thirty pounds. So they could afford it, true, though that was more than their regular Broadstairs holiday would cost. But the whole idea was disturbing. It would break an old custom, make a rift, Waggoner felt, in a pattern, which would never be the same again.

'Not us,' he said. It crossed his mind that it would be bad if Andy was going to start putting ideas into Agnes' head. But he must have seen that they didn't want it; nothing further was said on the subject, then or later, and if the idea had really penetrated Agnes' mind, then she had obviously put it out again, like the sensible person she was.

They wrote their customary letter booking their room, and two weeks later, as always, came the answer from Mrs. Moser, confirming it. It had occurred to Waggoner that perhaps they ought to offer to take Andy with them; but he left it to Agnes, who didn't seem to feel the necessity; so he naturally said nothing either.

As it turned out Andy was quite content to stay behind by himself, and had taken it for granted that he would, like his daughter. They were a family of flaccid bonds of affection.

'Be right as rain,' he assured Waggoner with a confident bob of the head, as they were leaving the house. What they would have done if the old man had shown distress Waggoner didn't care to think.

'He be all right?' Waggoner had asked Agnes, in the privacy of their bedroom. Both knew he meant, not only would Andy be able to fend for himself, but whether he would use and protect their house and property well in their absence.

'He will,' Agnes had answered positively. 'Very good about locking up behind him and putting things away he is. He's an old sailor, don't forget. . . . Used to managing,' she had elaborated.

Waggoner grunted, willing to believe her.

It had been a bit strange coming back to the house to find it alive, lived in, in contrast to former returns from holiday when all had been dank and dust-smelling, with the feel and stillness of emptiness. It was soon clear that not only had Andy looked after himself but had also kept the house in better-than-normal shape. Everything shone, sparkled, or glowed. In fact Waggoner wasn't sure that such perfection was entirely welcome: to him, because it was out of the ordinary, and to Agnes because it might convey some subtle criticism of her own care.

There was also, lurking, come upon unawares, in the folds of the curtains, in the broom-and-mackintosh cupboard under the stairs, in various nooks and crannies, a strange new smell. It was a faint and not displeasing smell of the tobacco the old man smoked in his pipe (though only in his room, in deference to the Waggoners' non-smoking); and a food smell: a good food smell.

It was definitely not the smell of the sort of food the Waggoners themselves liked. (The fare at Mrs. Moser's boardinghouse was just what Waggoner and Agnes relished: steak and chips, fish and chips, with the occasional flourish of fried liver and bacon and tomato). No; in this smell spices and flavourings had played a part, and what Agnes called 'messed up' cooking.

But the meal Andy had thoughtfully prepared and had waiting for them turned out to be some kind of a stew and though Waggoner of course approached it with caution it did in fact taste delicious. Delicious, that is, provided one didn't know what one was eating. . . . There appeared to be random small limbs and bits of meat and unfamiliar vegetables in a very thick broth. But he noticed that Agnes, after stirring her portion around with her spoon, had left it nearly all, as though to emphasise that her father's cooking wasn't to everyone's liking.

Later, Andy having gone out, Waggoner remarked that he'd kept the place quite well.

Agnes had sniffed for answer.

'What's the matter, then?' Waggoner was surprised.

'Nothing. . . . He did all right. . . . I told you he wouldn't be any trouble.'

Waggoner had meant that. 'That's what I was saying.'

'Yes, well . . . he hasn't got anything else to think of, like. All the time in the world, he's got.'

Yes, Waggoner agreed that Andy did have, but said no more, not understanding Agnes' defensiveness. She did seem put out, just when she ought to have been pleased. She'd get over it, whatever it was, though.

And so it was. The holiday was not so much forgotten as incorporated into the body of the practically identical ones which had gone before: holidays differing one from another only in the number of fine or rainy days and, this year, in the absence of one of the long-time regulars like themselves: a Miss Murvin from Croydon who, Mrs. Moser told them, had 'passed on' during the year.

It was a pity, but they could hardly have pretended grief. It was rather as though a building—a small shop or pub, for instance —which they had been used to passing regularly had been demolished. Something else would, undoubtedly, be put in its place.

And, indeed, the single room always occupied by Miss Murvin had been taken by a Mr. Proudfoot, who was a supervisor—what used to be called a floorwalker—in a department store. He was elderly, a widower, as he hastened to tell them, with grown and married daughters. He was neither more nor less interesting than Miss Murvin, which was to say that he was not really enthralling. Being new there were new facts to be observed in his looks and behaviour; but these were too unremarkable even to give the Waggoners anything to mention between themselves.

In fact Mr. Proudfoot merged so well into the background of the Pines—Mrs. Moser's house—that he might have been specially created out of all the world, in all the universe, for the express and only purpose of replacing, in bed and at board, the departed Miss Murvin. There was about him, if one came close enough, an odour as of well-preserved dust, characteristic of small, old-fashioned drapery shops which sell stout, hard-wearing stuff by the yard, together with tape, buttons, and elastic. Such shops as still exist—though as hard to find as birds of almost extinct species— are, like Mr. Hostace—clinging to a way of life already in the past, hoping to make them last as long as their own limited life expectancies.

Mr. Proudfoot had related all this to the Waggoners one night when it was raining and nobody had the heart to trudge the half mile to the pier, even to get the fresh air for which they had come to Broadstairs.

'What'll happen to you, then?' Agnes asked. 'When the shop closes down?' She was counting stitches on her needle and didn't

CHAPTER 7

A year went by on painful feet; Waggoner knew that Andy had been with them for more than a year because they went away to Broadstairs again; and Andy, who had looked after things just as well as the first time, had come round to their tastes more. The meal awaiting them on their return was grilled tomatoes on toast, which was the normal Sunday night supper. This time there was no exotic stew smell and perhaps the furniture wasn't polished more than usual. They had become used to the old man's pipe, so they didn't even notice that.

Naturally, Broadstairs hadn't suffered any sea change either. Mrs. Moser had a new set of false teeth, which one could hardly fail to notice as she ate in the dining room with the guests, and they clicked so loudly that you could hear them right across the room. Mr. Proudfoot looked rather more tattered round the edges —or perhaps it was simply the knowledge of his parlous circumstances which gave the impression.

Still, Waggoner was no longer concerned about him and had forgotten his quite irrational anxiety. Time, which for a brief flash had seemed to menace them both, had once more become, as it had always been before, a measure on clockfaces, so that one knew when to eat, when to leave the house in the morning or the office in the afternoon.

Time, of course, counted passing days too: it was a date on newspapers and on the office calendar, where there was a different picture for each month, each to a leaf, from the russet-tinged forests for the autumnal months, to skating people on jolly ponds and on to lucent springtime pools and leafy summer meadows—these supplied by the firm's insurance company. Time it was rather than temperature that dictated if Miss Hirsh wore a thick woolly cardigan and whether the current Amanda or Arabella or Melanie showed their bosoms through filmy gauze or outlined in tight sweaters.

The main delineation of the seasons was the varying character of the telly-programmes: rather boring old films of summer between long sequences of cricket and tennis, or the winter football matches and wildly, hysterically hilarious comics.

Time measured the onset of Christmas shopping (twenty-one days to:) and then there was, after the ritual of thinking about the summer holiday, the approach of Agnes' birthday, when Waggoner always bought her a black handbag. Then, in spring, there was their wedding anniversary, when they went out for the evening 'up west,' and pretended to each other that they enjoyed the spaghetti and grilled ham which they always ate before going on to see a musical show (which they could have seen, only better done, on telly at home) as both realised, but neither mentioned.

One year, greatly daring, after Agnes said she'd read about it in the papers, they ordered a dish called 'scampi' for their meal. It was very up-to-date, Agnes said and she wanted to see what all the fuss was about. In one of the weekly women's mags which she read some heroines had even surrendered to some unnamed and unmentionable sin after a meal of this food. But it was openly—and quite reasonably—priced on the menu of the big restaurant and turned out to be no more than small fried morsels which tasted like a combination of fish and chips and perhaps was. They agreed that this was an example of the silliness of all things modern and that the next year they would go back to the grilled ham again, even though they saw that it was now called 'gammon' and served on oval plates instead of round ones.

Time, then, was really quite a manageable concept, with its still smaller, homelier divisions: each day bounded by sleeping and waking, by going in and out. A day was a day and a night, and the night was margined with the hot drink (malt or chocolate-flavoured) and by breakfast, with boiled egg except on Sundays, when it was scrambled and partnered with a piece of bacon.

Mr. Fifterley was droning on and questioning a man Waggoner had never seen in his life . . .

As he listened he realised that the man was a doctor, another one. He'd done an autopsy, if you please! For what? For nothing! To find out nothing that Waggoner hadn't been anxious to tell them himself, at once, and for nothing. Whereas this man, as Waggoner could tell by the cut of his jib (an expression he must have picked up from Andy), would be in the ten-pounds-a-day class. Ten pounds he'd be costing the poor devils of rate and taxpayers, just to tell them what Waggoner knew and wanted to tell. If that didn't show you what nonsense all this was, then Waggoner didn't know what would!

The man had a square red face and he spoke without moving his slit of a mouth, inaudibly to Waggoner.

Waggoner wondered how he'd have felt about facing all this if he'd known in advance. He'd never imagined there'd be such a fuss and a going-on. He'd thought that once he'd said 'I did!' it would be much the same as when one said 'I do!' getting married. You owned up, accepted responsibility, and that was that. How wrong he'd been!

Still, as he'd thought, as he still saw it, he hadn't had any real alternative. His actions had been mapped out for him, each one following inevitably and without any will of his, from when he'd returned home one February night. . . . Of course, it had taken him time to read the map (some people never succeeded), but once he'd seen the way . . . well, there it was.

Of course it hadn't been night, unless you call six o'clock night because of the darkness and it being the day's end. The street-lamps were alight, at all events, each making a haloed moon in the damp misty air which was grey, really, rather than black. Waggoner had watched his own breath puffing out like those balloons in which the characters in comic strips speak or think.

> 'Moons, balloons,
> Shining like spoons
> Hanging like festoons
> In cartoons,'

59

Waggoner had versified, not caring that it wasn't very good, but in contented frame of mind himself because the cold and dreariness accentuated the approaching warmth and comfort of home. His feet throbbed with anticipation of ease like horses scenting the stable.

He'd had two newspapers under his arm, he remembered, both the evening papers, left behind by foolishly prodigal readers in the train.

It was beans-on-toast night, with later one of his favourite serials on telly. There were two cans of beer in the sideboard; he'd bought them after the new neighbours had visited and it had occurred to Waggoner that he ought to have offered them something. But they'd never come again, so the beer was still there. . . . Andy could have one if he was staying at home.

Waggoner snuffled. He'd had his bout of flu for the year, so wasn't really afraid of getting it again. A cold was nuisance enough, though. Agnes must have given it to him. She'd had flu when he did, though of course not as badly, which was just as well since she'd had to nurse him. . . . Now she had a cough which distracted him just when there was something on the telly he didn't want to miss; it had even kept him awake at night. He'd meant to tell her to buy herself some cough sweets to suck.

It was from the instant when, having extended his hand, his key, to open the front door and it had opened itself instead, before he could insert the key, that everything had begun to go wrong, utterly and irrevocably. Though even then he hadn't recognised it.

Andy had stood there, an Andy who appeared to have shrunk, suddenly and dramatically, his face yellow and a scared look about his eyes, with the lower lids somehow drooping and the rims red inside.

Agnes' death had been quite in keeping with Agnes alive. Apart from the disconcerting unpreparedness in which Waggoner found himself, she could scarcely have managed the matter with less inconvenience or more dispatch.

The doctor said it was a heart attack, probably brought on by neglected flu. Waggoner didn't believe this for a moment, but he was prepared to accept it. However, there was an inquest, which Waggoner had to attend, though he hadn't been asked to say anything. So even that hadn't been too bad, and they'd been quite understanding at the office, not even docking his pay for the two days he'd been away: one each for the inquest and the funeral.

Elmwood, Braine & Hostace had sent a wreath. It hadn't been a very pretty one: laurel leaves and some kind of orange-coloured berries. Still, he knew that February is deficient in flowers except for the very expensive, hot-house kinds, which one could hardly expect. There was another wreath, smaller, of 'everlasting' flowers, of subdued colours, from Miss Hirsh and Sharon. Miss Hirsh came to the funeral, too, which was strange and un-necessary, Waggoner thought.

Seeing her there in unfamiliar felt hat and black cotton gloves, Waggoner felt oddly disassociated. It was like getting one's dimensions mixed up, someone from another world, another time se-quence somehow strayed into one's own where they didn't belong. Miss Hirsh had so strayed (it would be unkind, if true, to say intruded) and Waggoner was uncomfortable about it.

Obviously, like anyone who dies other than by their own hands, Agnes had had no control over the time of her dying. Yet it had been considerately, expeditiously done. Not for her the hys-teria of accident, the excruciating martyrdom of the relatives of those incurably, lingeringly ill, with bedside scenes and hospital theatricality. She had simply subsided into that dark pool which embraces all humanity sooner or later, with typical decency and composure.

She had saved him worry and excitement and inconvenience— not to speak of possible expense. She had been there to serve him his breakfast in the morning as usual; but by evening, when she should have been giving him his beans on toast, she was no longer alive. It was part of the very Agnes-ness of her that she should have been there today and gone—not on the tomorrow— but by the very same evening. It was also due to her administering organizing hand reaching from the grave, an Agnes-originating bonus, that he was able, through Andy's presence, to continue his life with a minimum of rearrangement.

Of course Waggoner knew that Agnes could have had no foreknowledge, no intuition, nor had any such contingency in mind when she had been instrumental in bringing the old man to the house. Credit where credit was due, but no more, he thought; and he wasn't about to set up some kind of dead-wife worship, making her the kind of plaster idol which, he had observed, men widowed of useful wives were wont to do.

All the same the continuity which was so valuable to him was possible only because of Andy, and especially because Andy was the sort of man he was. Agnes had brought him the efficient, the self-effacing, domesticated handy-Andy.

As for Andy's own grief, if any, Waggoner saw little sign. True he no longer brought home the heavy, musty library books; but this was probably because he had less time on his hands, with all the housework to do. He may have missed Agnes and been a bit lonely; she would probably have been a kind of sheet anchor to him, replacing his own dead wife. With her gone he began, very gradually, to deteriorate: a large, shabby old man like an abandoned trawler, its moorings corroded, left to rust away and disintegrate because it wasn't worth anyone's while to care for them, or it.

The office once more became a humdrum humming background; Miss Hirsh, in normal daytime attire, was once more the Miss Hirsh he knew, not a stranger in unaccustomed outdoor clothes, intruding awkwardly into his private life. Anthea succeeded Sharon as tea-bearer, but soon left to become a 'temp,' for more money, as she told them. No one was really sorry because she had always had to keep one hand free to hold back her hair, so that the other, insufficient to the task, served everyone cold tea, slopped into the saucer from constant head-jerkings also needed to keep back the hair. She was replaced by Dolores, whose hair was, to everyone's relief, quite short, though worn in a frizzed-out, golliwogg style, which gave the impression that it must constantly be letting out particles of dust or fluff.

Andy had taken over the entire running of the house as unobtrusively as he did everything. Even the meals appeared in their ordained sequence and disposition. There were no more ill-advised stews and rarely a flavour or scent that Waggoner had not been used to for years.

Except in one particular Andy had not innovated or improved; and this exception, though making a great impression on Waggoner, was probably unconscious on the old man's part.

On the day after Agnes' funeral Waggoner was prepared to enter his own house as usual. As usual the key stuck slightly at the quarter turn; and this was followed by an infinitesimal retraction, then a full turn. All of this Waggoner did without any longer being aware of the manoeuvre but which, having been made, gave a subtle sense of satisfaction, of something accomplished as the door opened.

The hall smelt faintly—as was right, it being a Wednesday—of melting cheese, for it was Welsh rarebit night. Superimposed was a stronger than usual scent of furniture polish. Andy must be more liberal in its use than Agnes; Waggoner wondered whether to remark that it cost money, and reminded himself to give thought to reducing the amount of housekeeping money he allowed each week. There were only two of them now so it ought really only to cost two-thirds as much to live.

He was so used to stepping three paces into the hall to walk around his slippers before taking off his outdoor shoes that he had done so (the shoes unlaced, the first sigh of relief drawn, automatic as a heartbeat) without ever considering that the slippers would not have been placed there by a solicitous wifely hand.

But it was Andy, not Agnes, who had put them there, and Waggoner had taken one and a half paces too many. He might, as he had so often wished, have remained standing, simply slipping out of his shoes to step straight into the slippers. For there they were, *toes facing inwards,* obviating the need for the clumsy walk-around.

Andy might or might not have seen and noticed Agnes' mistake (which was really a natural one for a woman, who had never had slippers put ready for her, to make); but more likely he had merely put them as he, a man, a slipper-receiver by right of birth, would want them himself.

Another change: also, really, if one analysed it, for the better, took place in Waggoner himself, as a direct result of changed circumstances.

It had never occurred to Waggoner that bed was for anything other than for sleeping. Of course in the early years of marriage, this had followed the occasional 'bout,' as both he and Agnes thought of it, of sex. However, both had regarded this as a more or less routine duty, necessary to prove that they were normal adults; and Agnes had seemed as content to abandon the tiring and tiresome exercise as he had been himself. That bed could be enjoyed as a means of relaxation, that a man could lie simply for the joy of lying—limbs spread, eyes open or closed but in either case fixed on nothing, following thoughts that moved, random as clouds and as purposeless—all this was quite new to Waggoner.

Naturally, he still woke and rose as promptly as ever, at the first shrill of the alarm clock pushing himself upright, swinging his legs out and down and feet feeling for the slippers, at rest on the cold island of lino. On Saturdays he always slept one extra hour and two on Sundays and woke, though without the clock, exactly on time.

It was this new dimension of ease, the sheer physical ability to lie swastika-limbed, taking up all the double bed himself, that showed Waggoner the enfolding bliss and relish of simply lying. So that he wondered what would happen if the struggle to get himself up became more and more difficult every day (not easier with victory over self as the preachers of moral righteousness said); and one day he would lose the fight and never again be able to gird himself together, his disparate limbs needing armouring for sheer existence like an ancient warrior's for battle.

Further than this he dared not let his imagination stray: he dared not ask himself—what then? What if he simply lay for the rest of time? Would he become a vegetable in fact as in metaphor? Why should he not be a happy pensioner of the Submissive Society, which would certainly support him in such a state forever? Ought he, in fact, to bestir himself if his antipathy for the daily hustle had become an illness? Illness was subsidised and compensated and sympathised with by Society and he was therefore entitled to support.

These were scarcely thoughts or calculations, being present in Waggoner's mind only in embryo. They were the ghosts of thoughts yet to be clothed in practical form. For the time, for some months,

64

for the best part of a year after Agnes' death Waggoner continued to live and work very much as before, carried along by the momentum of all the preceding years. The past bore him along and there was no twist nor turn nor obstacle to divert him.

And so he might have continued forever and the world and Mr. Fifterley, Q.C., and the sniffy, mosquito-faced judge, and the twelve strangely assorted housewives and grocers and accountants and builders and whatever they were would never have heard of Waggoner, but for a stupid accident caused by the most trivial, incongruous object imaginable.

CHAPTER 8

Yes, it was clear to Waggoner that he would have gone on as a law-abiding citizen until the Old Age Pension (with some small supplement from Elmwood, Braine & Hostace) supplied his diurnal needs; until Meals on Wheels eventually brought food to his lap and the District Nurse put it into his mouth; and until he was eventually himself wheeled away into some kind of Retirement Home—which he pictured as similar to a field he had once seen on telly, where pensioned-off horses with sagging bellies cropped and nuzzled the rough, tufted grass with greying muzzles. So his bodily requirements would be cared for; and in the end, he supposed, a state-appointed undertaker would measure him and put him away, snugly packaged, to Rest in Peace until the Last Trump was sounded by a fully paid-up member of the Musicians' Union.

It was ironic that so much meticulous planning for Waggoner's welfare had been disrupted by an accident happening to someone else: that it had been a banana skin on which Andy slipped, as if proving the validity of the trite old jokes; and especially because Andy hated bananas, calling them monkey fruit and avoiding them as though prescient.

Waggoner shrugged, acknowledging the blindness of fate. As punctuation to the post-mortem report the gesture seemed to a bored young reporter to show Waggoner's callousness and contempt. He was the only journalist sitting out the trial, which was so unlikely to yield the shocks for which the public was assumed to be avid. He shaped a sentence, then a colourful paragraph, which he was already experienced enough to know would be cut out by a sub, which he owed it to his muse to write.

The old man had been to the market, buying frugally and economically instead of picking up packaged items from the supermarket conveyor belt. He'd stepped off the curb and slipped; tried to get up and couldn't. He'd been carried off to the hospital and X-rayed and by the time Waggoner came home that evening, instead of his slippers, toes pointing inwards, he found a sympathetic policeman to tell him that Andy had a fractured thigh.

Waggoner went round to see the old man that evening. Andy wasn't in pain now, or at least he said he wasn't. They'd set the bone and pinned it together, he thought, and it was in plaster. Waggoner could see a hilly hump beneath the red blankets. Andy seemed almost proud, as though of an achievement.

'Just went from under me they did,' he said of his legs. 'There I was one minute, just like always. Stepped aside, y'see, round this pile of boxes. And the next thing . . . ! He shook his head, blue eyes glinting at the wonder of it.

'Oh, ar,' Waggoner sympathised, also shaking his head, clutching the bunch of draggled Michaelmas daisies he'd bought outside the hospital, because one couldn't go in empty-handed.

They'd let him come home as soon as the plaster was properly set, Andy had understood, though of course no one had actually told him anything clearly.

Still, he seemed quite well, really, and Waggoner went away more or less satisfied, ready to stand temporary upset. It might take some days: even a week. He realised that. But afterwards there was no reason why things shouldn't resume their normal pattern. It was a nuisance, of course, but Waggoner would manage.

He left the hospital after a seemly half hour, lips pursed in a soundless whistle in time to the words forming in this mind:

> Hobble bobble
> He slipped on a cobble,
> But I'll have no trobble. . . .

No, that wasn't good enough. He tried again, and now it went with a swing:

> Hobble bobble
> Slip and spin
> Andy on banana skin.

Who threw it there?
It was a sin!
But when he's able
Again to hobble
Waggoner won't have much . . . trobble.

Well, the final rhyme was a bit feeble, but no matter. He
was in a good mood, a reaction to the initial shock and fear.
He even contemplated dropping into the Fox and Feathers as he
went past it going home. After all, he'd have something to tell.
It wasn't every day one was involved with police, ambulances,
and emergency operations.

However, when it came to it, Waggoner hesitated outside the
pub and then decided against it. He didn't know anyone there
and wasn't any good at starting conversations with strangers.
Home, even without anyone there to do things for him, was best;
he didn't mind being alone.

As the word came into his mind, he realised that all the
'trobble' with the rhyme had been because he'd used the word
'cobble,' which was not only difficult but unnecessary, being in-
accurate. Now 'stone' rhymed with many more words . . .

And Waggoner won't be alone!

A perfect last line!

For a week Waggoner was able to carry on without suffering
any serious inconvenience. Anything in the house that wasn't
directly connected with his own food he left alone. He knew that
there had to be cleaning and washing and washing-up; but Andy
would have to bestir himself a bit more when he got home, that
was all.

It was summertime, summer weather, and that helped, of
course. In the office nothing changed. The uncleaned windows
screened out the brightness of any sunlight; in the winter, although rain sluiced the glass, leaving it speckled-clean, the light
was dimmer, so it was impossible from inside to say what time
of the year it was, what season, any more than one could here,
in the court.

Waggoner related the story of Andy's fall several times, between

69

sips of tea: to Fogg, the 'junior,' who wasn't often there, being busy with mysterious 'outside' work. He listened intently, picking at a pimple on his chin, shook his head, and disappeared, to go to the customs, so he said, returning just before closing time exuding a rich smell of whiskey, and noticeably more cheerful. Miss Hirsh and Dolores, as well as sympathetic tongue-clicks, asked helpful and fruitful questions. For instance, there was the responsibility, to be discussed at length, of the person who had thrown the banana skin away so recklessly. But obviously, the miscreant being unknown, and unlikely to be found, this was not very productive. It was not, as Waggoner pointed out, like when they left a cockroach in a milk bottle, or baked beetles into cakes: then you knew who to claim against.

It appeared that Dolores was enthralled by anything to do with hospitals; she admitted it, blushing, so she must have entertained romantic dreams connected with doctors. She offered at once to go with Miss Hirsh, or without her, to visit the old man. Waggoner protested that it wasn't necessary, though he knew that the gregarious Andy would enjoy it. Deep down, he was aware of jealousy, for he was really the one who needed and deserved the feminine fussing.

By the end of the third week when Andy had still not come back, the house was becoming more and more of a mess. Waggoner had gone on piling up used clothes, the shirts, towels, and dishcloths which, all his life, had always vanished from his view and out of his ken as soon as soiled. He had never given thought to such things; his job was to earn a living, which he did. As he now continued to add to the overflowing linen basket in the bathroom, the heaps on the upstairs landing and that in the kitchen, the house was beginning to look quite sordid.

His consolation, that Andy would be home any day, was wearing thin. Waggoner paid another visit to the hospital (actually his third—he had been quite assiduous).

Andy—as Agnes had said—had the capacity of adapting himself. He seemed ominously at home in the hospital ward, in the white bed, from which the hump had disappeared: a good sign, as Waggoner supposed. He also looked quite well himself: above the white cotton nightshirt his face glowed like an autumn apple, russet-red. He was on first-name terms with everyone around, full of gossip and chatter, more animated, really, than he had ever been at home.

He seemed limitlessly interested in his fellow-sufferers. All appeared to be elderly men, though of some no more was to be seen than beaked noses pointed up to the ward ceiling. All the beds were looped around with pipes attached to bottles from which liquids dripped into the old men, or into which they continually distilled exudations like trees tapped for precious saps. There was none of the proverbial hospital smell that Waggoner had expected, and which he had supposed would be an exciting combination of ether or chloroform and disinfectant. But there was only a faintly disagreeable odour which he couldn't identify (or hoped he could not); and concluded that being the Health Service, They wouldn't be able to afford disinfectant. Perhaps they used some kind of gas nowadays for the operations, also.

'Didn't it hurt? When they set your leg?' he asked Andy.

'No. Not then. Not at all, really. But it was those X-rays I didn't like.'

'X-rays? They don't hurt, do they?'

'No . . .' The blue eyes were the colour of that stuff his mother had had a brooch out of: butterfly wings, she'd said. Momentarily they clouded; then gleamed again. 'But near frightened me out of me wits, though. Dang great thing, big as the roof of a house it was, hanging up there. And they pushed me in under it. . . . Thought for a minute they were going to operate on me with it; something like that. Squash me to death, they could've. Scared the . . . frightened me, that did,' Andy said, with relish for his own distress now that it was past. 'Nobody told me, not till after, what it was they were doing. But then I thought: "Here goes, Andy Matthews! Here come the bug-eyed monsters to torture you," I thought. And that cheered me up, like, and I was all right after that. Then I saw X-RAY ROOM written up outside it, and I knew then.'

Waggoner stared at him.

'It was imagination, see?' Andy clarified.

Waggoner didn't see. 'They ought to have told you,' he said.

71

'Aye. They ought that.'

'There ought to be a letter.'

'Letter?'

'To the papers . . . complaining. People should complain about anything like that. It isn't right. Might've given you a heart attack. Then the Health Service would have been to blame,' Waggoner said indignantly.

'If I were dead, wouldn't no one have known why,' Andy said philosophically.

'Might've done for you,' Waggoner persisted.

'Well it didn't, then.' Andy had shrugged it off; and this reminded Waggoner about the banana-skin thrower. But the old man wasn't really responsive about that either. 'Find 'em first,' he opined. 'Can't, can you? And there's no law.'

'Isn't there?'

'Couldn't be,' Andy said. 'Could there?'

'It says up: "Penalty five pounds,"' Waggoner said doggedly. 'For throwing litter. If banana skins aren't litter I don't know what is.'

'Where's it say that?'

Waggoner couldn't remember any exact spots, not to name, but he knew he'd seen the notice. 'They don't have: "Don't Spit" or "Don't steal" up,' he said. 'But it's against the law just the same. They don't have to have it everywhere.'

'Well, but they don't go after you,' Andy said. 'Not for spitting and littering and the like. . . . Keep 'em at it all the time, wouldn't it? Then there'd have to be a case. Never be finished.'

The patient in the next bed, an old man whose parchment face was covered in white prickles like an ancient hedgehog, snored in unconsciousness. He was more wreathed about in bottles and tubes than anyone else. 'He was operated this morning,' Andy explained. 'It's the kidneys. Always bad, that; and it's what gives first: the Works and the Parts. You know.'

Waggoner didn't know and would have preferred not to, but Andy went into details with some evident relish so that he was quite glad when a starched nurse came in ringing a little dinner bell, which meant that visiting time was over.

Andy gave another parting promise that he would be home in a week.

The one who really ought to have been sitting up here in the dock was the banana-skin thrower, of course, not Waggoner. But no! He was off somewhere, no doubt enjoying himself, not knowing how he'd thrown the equivalent of a spanner into the workings of other peoples' lives. Scot free he was, while Waggoner . . .

> 'Quite foot-loose
> And fancy-free
> But put the skids
> Under Andy and me,'

Waggoner muttered, going home that evening.

The man (Waggoner had always pictured the villain as a man, though he had no proof that it was) probably spent his time standing at some machine in a factory, holding some tool against a whirling wheel which peeled steel slivers from it: Waggoner had seen such processes many times on telly where it was some kind of picture symbol for a worker. Perhaps, though, the peeling accounted for the man's carelessness. Habit, in a way.

In a way, too, Waggoner had the laugh over him at the end, though. He was still out there, battling away, and anyone who had to stand all day at a machine must really suffer from his feet. Then, on his way home, he'd have to rack his brains whether to do the shopping before he got his train (and having to squeeze himself and his loaded basket through the swaying, crowded corridors), or wait till arrival at the home station and chance the shops being closed or having no more cut bread.

While he, Waggoner . . . From the corner of his eye Waggoner stole a glance at Mr. Parson's rounded, pregnant-looking belly. Mr. Parsons and his colleagues—up and down the ladder of authority and administration—had the problems of logistics connected with Waggoner.

It was up to Them now!

Waggoner shifted—wriggled, you would really have to call it—on the wooden chair. The warder sitting on the other side of him from Mr. Parsons (who ignored his fidgeting, apparently couldn't

73

care) leaned across and whispered to Waggoner. But he said no; it was all right. The movement had been expressing the subconcious pleasure he'd felt at how he was to be looked after. . . .

Like now: this was an example. This chap was actually concerned (it was his business to be concerned) about whether Waggoner wanted to go to the toilet. . . . 'Toilet' They called it inside; he'd have to remember that.

Waggoner glanced, acknowledging thanks at the man, who was rotund, with a puddingy face with kind lines on each side of pink, pursed lips. He'd always thought warders were great hefty wrestler-type chaps. . . . But of course they wouldn't need ones like that for him.

This warder's name was Owens . . . Mr. Owens. Waggoner preferred him to Mr. Parsons, though he hardly knew any of them very well. Not that it mattered; he'd soon be going where there'd be quite a different set. You couldn't imagine this lot in a real prison, with tough types!

Still, warders were all right, Waggoner had seen. He'd known it was so: as long as you were all right to them they had to treat you right. . . . They even called him Mr. Waggoner. They had to, because he was still being tried.

Waggoner sighed and, recalling himself in time, restrained another wriggle, this time one of exasperation. It was hard to remain patient; but he supposed they had to earn their money . . . even Mr. Fifterley. Had to show they were doing something for it.

Waggoner wondered how much They were paying him, and thought that it couldn't help being too much!

It was all such a farce, he thought again, as so often he had in these days, and lapsed into memories of how he had landed in the middle of it all, to be the focus of it: poor old John Aldous Waggoner, who hadn't bargained for anything of the sort. . . .

CHAPTER 9

Waggoner gave a silent whistle of astonishment when Doris Groundling walked into the witness-box. She had been called by the Crown, of course. . . . Yes, the man about to question her was the one who sat behind the prosecutor: a lean, grey man rather frighteningly unnoticeable. Waggoner had been only peripherally aware of him, a shadow between the exuberant Fifterley and the august Mr. Whitely, Q.C., his 'leader.'

But what were they doing, then? Working in relays? Was that fair? It didn't seem to be. Waggoner knew that they did that in brainwashing so that the victim (Fifterley) would be worn out while the inquisitors remained fresh and vigorous.

But if Fifterley was an object for pity he seemed unaware of it. He was leaning back—almost lying, really—in his chair, which was canted so that it looked impossibly balanced on its hind legs. His eyes were closed, so you might think, for deepest concentration, though Waggoner suspected that he was merely resting his eyes, or even dozing.

When Doris Groundling was asked how old she was, Waggoner felt quite a quiver of joy. She would have to tell the truth; and when she answered it was in a voice so muted that the grey man had to repeat the question, and even the judge, who usually kept his eyes down on his table, looked up at her from beneath wrinkled brows, so that they almost disappeared into his wig.

So she was forty-seven, was she? Waggoner would have given her five more, for luck.

But he waited with some curiosity as to what she could possibly say about him. The Groundlings had hardly known the Waggoners (not that they wouldn't have liked to know more, being nosey, so Waggoner considered); but the fact remained that they didn't.

What can the Groundlings know of Waggoners who scarcely Groundlings know? Waggoner really wondered. Had Mrs. Groundling made up some story, out of spite? Because Agnes and he hadn't wanted to waste their time with her and her husband?

But probably she'd have had no choice. She'd have had to give evidence for the Crown if They told her, wouldn't she? Waggoner wasn't sure. It was a point he'd never thought to ask Mr. Nowditch, nor Nowditch to mention . . . not that it mattered!

Waggoner's one encounter with the couple had been so surprising as to be almost shocking. It wasn't that either of them were at all repulsive, nor even unusual in any way. It was just that the Waggoners had never had an unannounced, unexpected visit before, nor many of any other sort for that matter.

He'd come home one evening (in autumn it was, the first hazy early-evening night of the year) thinking of nothing much but remembering for some reason that when he and Agnes had first moved to Pontefract Crescent there had been a muffin-man coming round at this time of day. Of course it was already a rarity, even then, but nice, really. He'd carried a tray on his head, and carried a small bell, which he rang, slowly, dolefully, in time to his cry: 'Mu-uufins! Hot muffins!' In fact the muffins were cold and you had to toast them yourself. Today, such was progress, the muffin-man could have been prosecuted under some law or other for making false claims. And, anyway, muffins were sold already wrapped in cellophane packets, nice and clean and without having been exposed to the muffin-man's fingers or the night air.

There used to be a baker delivering bread, too; and gipsies selling clothes-pegs, wooden ones like miniature dolls; and surely it was at this time of year the Bretons used to come round, going from door to door with strings of onions round their necks? Lots of people had come selling their wares; but it must have been a nuisance to householders, since many gates had little enamel signs: NO HAWKERS. So the hawkers, the muffin-men and the Bretons and the gipsies, had turned their talents to other activities, or had simply died off, and instead there were men who drove up in cars and sold vacuum cleaners and encyclopaedias and were called salesmen.

Meditating on such matters, Waggoner arrived at his own gate, and had actually entered his front door, had one foot poised for the shoe to be unfastened, before he became aware of voices from the front room. Reluctantly, deciding against the slippers for the moment, he went in.

A man and woman were seated vis-à-vis at the table. Agnes fluttered uncharacteristically. 'This is my husband, Mr. Waggoner,' she announced. 'Er . . . This is Mr. and Mrs. Groundling. They've come to live next door.'

Waggoner couldn't see that that was any reason why they should overflow into his house, but the man bobbed up (he was that kind of man, short, tight-packed into his skin, ruddy, bouncing like a ball) and seized Waggoner's flaccid hand and shook it.

'Dick!' he announced. 'Dick and Doris! Since we're neighbours we won't stand on ceremony. I said to Doris, I said: "We'll go and call on those nice people next door," I said, "before we do anything else. We have to get to know them to borrow their lawn mower!"' And he roared with laughter.

Waggoner was bewildered. 'We haven't got any lawn mower, Mr.—Grounsel.' Was the man mad?

'Groundling, Groundling! No, that's the joke! I know; I saw! You haven't got any lawn, either.' This time they both laughed. 'Dick and Doris, remember? But Groundling's the name: it's historic.' He turned to Agnes, who perhaps struck him as more impressionable. 'Grand, that means big. Ground—grand. And ling's a fish . . . a big fish, that's me!'

Nervously, Agnes pushed forward on the table a plate of biscuits. They were the kind called 'squashed-fly' because of the raisins, and were favourites of Waggoner, who liked them with his night-time drink. He saw that Agnes had already made them tea and wondered how long they'd been here and when they'd go home. . . . Lawn mower, indeed!

'We just came a little while ago,' Doris Groundling said, as though she had read his thoughts, which would not have been hard. 'We didn't want to be a nuisance. . . . We thought we'd catch you before you began your tea.'

She was an improbably blond blonde, dessicated, thin and, even seated, it was obvious that she was taller than her husband.

'Yes,' Waggoner said. 'That's when I . . . come home.' He now saw with distaste that she had on her lap a very small, very hairy dog. It was regarding him through its fringe with a beady eye.

'Sweet, isn't she?' Doris Groundling said.

Both Waggoners nodded, without conviction.

'Perhaps you don't like dogs, though?'

'Oh no,' Agnes protested, somewhat feebly. 'It's all right.' Waggoner shook his head. But it was a lie, for though he'd never had anything to do with animals he was sure that the distrust and even enmity he felt for them would be mutual.

'We haven't any kids, see,' Doris went on. 'Neither have you, have you?'

The Waggoners shook their heads.

'Thought so,' Doris Groundling confirmed. "You can always tell.'

Waggoner supposed she meant that the house wouldn't be so tidy; but then children would hardly have been in this, the front room.

Front rooms were meant for guests, and as the Waggoners had none and they had decided that the room was too cold, they had never bothered to heat it. Like the hall it still had the decoration put up by the previous tenant: the lower half of the walls covered with an early forerunner of plastics called Lincrusta, a hard-wearing, glossy material embossed with a design of pineapples and acorns, arranged in vertical stripes. This Agnes had had painted over in its original chocolate brown, which didn't show dirt; the upper part was distempered in yellow, for brightness, though this had faded to buff-grey. On the mantelpiece, above the brown-tiled aperture for a stove, was a vase some helpless relative had given them for a wedding present. It contained a parchment fly swatter and three bullrushes.

'If you ask me,' Doris Groundling said (though no one had), 'a dog is better. A child: what do you get? Trouble, that's all. You've only got to look at the people who've got them to see. And as for company . . . don't make me laugh! There's none of them company like my little Annabelle here.' And she patted the dog, which turned an elfin snarl towards her.

'Only give her a bit of liver and she's happy,' Dick Groundling confirmed. 'Doesn't take much.'

'She thinks I'm God and a marrow bone all in one, don't you, precious?' Doris kissed the dog somewhere between its moustache and the pink bow holding up a cockscomb between its ears. It growled softly. 'If once in a while she forgets her manners and makes a weeny little puddle on the carpet, well, I smack her little bottom and put her outside and she knows. And she doesn't hate me for it and have one of those traumas you're always hearing about, or get her sexes all mixed up and have to murder someone for it.'

Dick Groundling, it transpired, was what he called a waste-disposal technician, which as further enquiry elicited meant that he was a plumber. Plumbers were manual workers, not even trades-men, and this would have presented Waggoner with a problem of some complexity if he had intended to carry on the acquaintance. The Groundlings were definitely on a lower social level than he, a clerk, even though he knew that in the topsy-turvy world of today the man would certainly earn far more than he did. Which was another reason for keeping yourself to yourself amid such per-plexing cross-currents.

Doris told them that she had been a 'model.' Waggoner thought this meant the kind of model who sits for artists, with or without a piece of gauze draped across their knees, and was startled, until she explained that it was clothes. 'In my young days, of course.' She fluttered eyelashes stiff as brushes over eyes like two pale blue marbles.

'Heh heh!' Dick Groundling guffawed. The Waggoners smiled politely, though neither could see what joke had been intended.

'Model!' Agnes had commented sniffily to Waggoner later, when they were alone. 'Mannequin was what they called it when she was working at it. If ever she was.'

'But what did they *want?*'

Agnes shrugged. 'Coming new to these parts they'd want to be friendly with next door.'

'Would they?' It was a new idea to Waggoner, who couldn't imagine himself setting out deliberately to visit total strangers because they happened to live in the next house. Nor, for that matter, visiting at all.

'People do,' Agnes went on, unusually informative. Perhaps the muscles of conversation, having been exercised, were now limber for use.

'Why?'

'To talk . . . company. Maybe beer. We ought to have given them beer.'

'We haven't got any. We never keep it.' Waggoner was perplexed.

'I know.'

The next day on his way home Waggoner had, rather shamefacedly, bought three cans of beer and placed them in the sideboard, where they companioned such exotic and unessayed luxuries as a jar of ginger (sent by Andy long ago from some far-off shore and which neither of them had liked enough to eat more than the first bit); a flask-sized bottle of brandy, kept for emergencies; and a tin which had once contained biscuits, in which Agnes kept carefully rolled-up bits of string.

However, Waggoner might have spared himself the trouble and the cash since the Groundlings never came again nor, not being invited, had the Waggoners returned the visit.

> It's rather queer
> To come for beer
> Make a special visit;
> And when you find
> It isn't there . . .
> That's not quite nice
> Now, is it?

was Waggoner's half apologetic rhyme on the subject. He realised that he and Agnes were perhaps a little lacking in sophistication; but still, he had nothing he wished to say to Dick Groundling, nor to hear from him. And he only hoped that Doris, with her patent-leather shoes and handbag and make-up, didn't give Agnes any ideas, unlikely as that seemed.

Fortunately, the brief encounter had no adverse effects: indeed, as Doris Groundling was trying to explain, the two families really had no contact. But she was managing to sound devious on account of what she called politeness, which meant avoidance of any direct statement. She also had a studied way of speaking, elocuting the words, sculpting them with her mouth as though they were to be spewed forth as chewing-gum art forms.

The lean grey individual, rocking back and forth as all the lawyers did, was asking in a tone of pained patience, as one determined to pry the truth from a reluctant source: 'And are you saying, then, that it was Mrs. Waggoner who ran . . . who ordered the affairs of the household? Or the prisoner?'

'I . . . I wouldn't know, would I? From the once?'

'But you must have had some indication? After all, any such unusual situation would be quite plain, would it not?'

Doris Groundling tilted her head to indicate deep thought as some extroverted dogs do. 'No,' she conceded at last. 'No, I wouldn't say that. . . . Not that I'd *know* anything, though.'

Mr. Fifterley rocked his chair so that it landed him on his feet. 'M'lud. . . . The witness has already said . . . And her *opinion* was asked, m'lud.'

The judge peered at the prosecutor. 'I don't er . . . quite see: this line of questioning?'

The grey man smiled sourly. 'I am anticipating my learned friend, m'lud.'

'Oh, ar, hrmph . . .' The judge waved a permissive hand and Fifterley turned a surrendering palm upwards. For all Waggoner could understand of this charade they might all be acting out one of those new plays which, as some people had said on telly, don't mean anything except to the actors who make them up as they go along. The questioning went on, mysterious in intent as before.

'But slight as your acquaintance, little as you knew them, you did live next door to these people, in a house with a common inside wall . . .'

'Pardon?' Doris Groundling was affronted.

'Your houses adjoined?'

'Oh! Well, yes. I suppose so; yes.'

'So you must at least be able to tell us, after this fairly close proximity of some years, whether you at any time suspected that this man, your neighbour, John Aldous Waggoner, was in any way mentally unstable?'

'Er . . . Not to say unstable: no.'

'Quite normal, you considered, then?'

'I—er . . .'

'M'lud!' It was Mr. Fifterley on his feet again. 'The witness . . .'

But this time there was a negative twitch of the woolly hood. The grey man smiled and repeated the question, and Doris Groundling was heard to say that, no, she hadn't ever thought there was anything peculiar about Waggoner, nor had her husband, come to that. 'A bit stingy, we thought it was, that's all. Keeping to themselves: old-fashioned. But we didn't mind. It takes all sorts.'

So it had been the beer—or rather the lack of it, Waggoner thought!

Then it was Fifterley's turn to ask her what sounded like the same questions another way round.

'You had the impression that *Mrs.* Waggoner would have been prepared to be friendly? Neighbourly in a normal fashion?'

'Oh yes. Yes, she would,' Doris Groundling said. Waggoner was amused. Little she knew!

'But it was the prisoner, *Mr.* Waggoner, who insisted on the couple's isolation?' Fifterley pressed.

'I suppose so, then. Must have been, mustn't it?'

'Their isolation from everyone, not only you, their next-door neighbours?'

Waggoner wished that Fifterley would stop trying so hard. Hadn't he grasped the fact that Waggoner *didn't want freedom?* That the last thing Waggoner wanted was a verdict of Not Guilty . . . if, indeed, that could be given by any sane jury?

Waggoner had heard people on the telly giving their opinion that God is Dead. He didn't know about that, and wasn't interested, because he didn't consider it his business. But what he did think was that Freedom is Slavery! He wanted to be free of Freedom. If Fifterley hadn't grasped that by now (and, after all, Waggoner had told him in as many words), then he was a bigger fool than he looked, which was scarcely possible!

Fifterley's ears were large and appeared to be functionally

moulded to catch sounds: words in this instance. And yet Waggoner had the impression that all he'd said to him passed across and over and round his head, like those isobaric patterns to which the weathermen pointed with such pride but which, affecting or even responsible for the climate of the countries, were really invisible and didn't exist at all. Waggoner thought that whether he protested innocence or guilt would make no difference to Mr. Fifterley, nor change either his opinion—if he bothered to have one—or his tactics. He seemed simply determined to go through a routine for which he was employed: the express purpose of which was to force Freedom-Slavery on Waggoner!

CHAPTER 10

Waggoner's slippers remained where he left them each night, in his bedroom; so he had a weary trek upstairs to get them, with his corns and bunions hurting like the very devil; and of course in the mornings it was impossible to remember, he had too much on his mind, to think of taking them down with him.

Sometimes he'd walk around downstairs in stockinged feet. He had to admit to himself that there was an exquisite delight in this: much more comfortable, much freer-feeling even than with the slippers. But mingled with that was a subconscious nagging. He knew that going barefoot was done by the sort of men who wore shirt sleeves and braces at home, ate fish and chips from a shop and had their beer fetched from a pub by children with runny noses.

He knew all this because his mother, who had brought him up in a neighbourhood where such behaviour was normal, had taught him to avoid and abhor it. His father had disappeared into some unexplained limbo (dead or alive, his mother had never said, and Waggoner hadn't been curious); but she had earned them a 're-spectable' living as a home-dressmaker for the better-off ladies around. It was she who had pushed him on to become a clerk in-stead of, say, a carpenter or mason. He'd had to live up to Mum, and always had, till now. He knew she'd frown at the stockinged feet and tell him it wasn't nice; but he really couldn't help it.

And anyway his mother had had 'ideas above her station': so at least he had heard her own mother say when that terrifying ancient crone had come to their house, the once that Waggoner could remember seeing her. After that (he had been quite small then and had taken everything literally) he had for a long time carried about a mental picture of his mother seated, demurely, hands folded in aproned lap, on one of those slatted benches they have in railway stations, with the name of the station written above her on a big shiny board. And still higher, in a floating bubble like the ones in comics, was written the word 'IDEAS!' in bold, flashing letters.

Dr. Kurt Jugend-Phipps, the head-shrinker that Fifterley had arranged for, had questioned Waggoner rather a lot about all that. Frankly, as he'd told the man, he'd forgotten this incident, and nearly everything else about his childhood until he was asked.

Dr. Jugend-Phipps had a nervous tic, an occasional twitch of the head (which, when you came to think of it, was odd for one in his profession); otherwise he looked the sort of man, like Fifterley, who would eat a large steak every day, play golf on weekends, and give opinions with which no one would dare to argue on the telly, between sips of what looked like water but was probably gin. He had a very carefully cultivated accent, which sounded like the perfect one you hear from carefully cultivated foreigners: in fact he had been born in Wimbledon.

'How old were you when your mother died?' he had asked Waggoner, unwrapping and lighting a very thin, black cigar, which added to the foreign impression.

'I don't know.'

'Don't know?'

'No.'

'You mean,' the doctor interpreted, speaking slowly and even more meticulously than before, 'you mean you don't know her age at death?'

'No. I mean I don't know when she died.'

Waggoner hadn't seen his mother since he'd left school and got a job which supported him. He'd never cared for her and, until the doctor asked him that, too, he'd never even considered whether she loved him or not.

He supposed she must have done; mothers did love their children, didn't they? She'd looked after him all right, and taught him to get on in the world. She'd been a hard worker herself: his lasting memory of her from childhood was of her dressing-gown chest stuck with pins like a pin cushion, as, spare needle in her mouth, she sewed away. He'd seen her on her knees, too, chalking along the hem of a dress being tried on in the front room by one of the 'ladies.'

He'd done his part, running out to buy sewing cotton or lengths of tape and delivering the finished gowns. Once the fishmonger's wife had asked him into the house and had given him a penny. There was a bowl of fruit on the sideboard with a couple of peaches on it. The sight and smell of these spelt luxury and riches to Waggoner for the rest of his life. He had never eaten a peach, feeling obscurely that they were out of his reach.

It wasn't so much tiredness as sheer discouragement that caused Waggoner to let things go about the house. Of course there was no one there but himself and, after all, it was for only a short while. As the plates and cups and saucers he'd used began to form piles and then towers that toppled, he found that you can, if you want, use the same cup several times over, and even some plates too. He felt a sneaking enjoyment of the small cheating (of Mum and, yes, of Agnes too). The very fact that it worked so well was depressing. What had all the Mums and Agneses to show for their years and years of religiously washing up breakfast and supper and dinner dishes when, come the next day they had to start all over again, just as though they hadn't done it at all?

This small conundrum rather haunted Waggoner for a day or two, with its implication of wasted lives: his own, too, come to that, doing over and over the same thing which also left nothing to show. . . .

Miss Hirsh must have noticed something: perhaps that Waggoner was looking untidy, even scruffy or downright neglected, for he had been forced to wear shirts which had been worn several times already and which he had withdrawn from the heap, waiting Andy's attention, on the bathroom floor.

'A man alone,' she said, 'I know how difficult it must be. I could come along one evening with you: tidy up. Put things in order. I could even take the washing down to the launderette. I quite like that, really. You get to know people while you're waiting there.'

'Er . . . thanks,' Waggoner had answered and, lying, quick as thought, instinctively, 'It's all right, really. The neighbour . . . while I'm out . . .'

'Oh!'

Miss Hirsh sounded disappointed, though logically there was no reason why she should be; she was not going to have to drudge in a stranger's house, though with credit for having offered. 'In that case, of course . . .' She pushed out of sight a shoulder strap that had strayed across her collarbone. 'If you're sure?'

Waggoner assured her that he was sure. His lie had been in response to a built-in alarm signal; though it wasn't till later that he'd recognised the impulse. Miss Hirsh had made her offer when, by rare chance, the two of them had been alone in the office. And there had been a strange coyness, never before noticed, in her manner.

For the first time he realised that to her he was no longer the dim, background figure he had been in the past, but was now changed, butterfly from grub, into an eligible widower. But she, alas, was still to him as she had always been: every part and detail fixed, *there,* much as the sky was, or the less ephemeral pattern of streets, pavements, roads, houses, railway stations, bridges and tunnels, stairs and lifts, and his own front garden path that he traversed every day. She was Miss Hirsh, face blurred by familiarity (so that he could no more have described it than he could his own), unseen beneath the bush of hair, above the bosom dowdily covered in unremarkable fabrics.

That this bosom (which, now that he came to think of it was in many respects like his mother's, seeming to be shaped from putty or plasticine, but certainly not of human tissue), should harbour within itself an inwardness, a wish to be other than it was, was astounding to Waggoner; so also the thought that Miss Hirsh should desire to be other than a two-dimensional figure in the backdrop of his days. None of this had remotely occurred to Waggoner before.

When it was brought home to him by Miss Hirsh's offer and by a certain glint in her eye, his first reaction, fortunately, was for escape. Then he reminded himself that in future he must take better care of his appearance. Scruffiness must never again be allowed to rouse maternal or perhaps the eternal, never-dead connubial hopes beneath that lace modesty!

In the kitchen at home, Waggoner scrambled about in regions where he had never even looked before, and discovered a large plastic bowl, strawberry-ice-cream-pink. In this, with water warmed in the kettle, he clumsily sloshed a couple of the dirtiest of his shirts and then hung them to dry draped over a chair back in the cat-smelling garden; there they became grimed before dried, with sooty droppings from ivy and foetid weeds and floating smudges from burning rubbish heaps. Later, though, he ironed them, but unsuccessfully, finding creases coming where he didn't put them and not where he meant them to be.

Still, he consoled himself that this, anything, was better than the ministrations of Miss Hirsh; and in any case it was all only temporary. Soon, any day, Andy would be back, and then his physical needs would be attended to as always.

In the meantime he did his best. On his way home he would do his shopping, hunting moodily around the small corner grocery, which had transformed itself into a supermarket by dint of dismissing its one assistant, stocking its eatables on open shelves in plastic bags, ready weighed and marked, and having the owner seated at a turnstile, in charge, by the door. Waggoner bought himself bacon and a tin of beans; but found when he reached home that he had neither bread nor butter.

Waggoner knew that there were organizations meant for coping with just such difficulties as those he was suffering. It was clear to him (as it must be to them) that if he was to carry on his function in society, to continue his job, fulfilling his quota of work: files neatly in rank, in seried order in cabinets, available on demand, together with office stationery, ledgers, typewriter erasers, and Attendance Record, then it was equally up to Them to see that he was able to manage when things went wrong at home.

He reckoned that, as a solid citizen who paid taxes and rates and went to work every day instead of drawing benefits, he had the right in return to demand, for instance, that the fire brigade would turn out, bells ringing and lights flashing, if his house caught fire, and that the police would come, equally visible and audible if he needed them. Surely, then, in a situation just as pressing, if, admittedly less urgent, he could expect help: an attendant—without lights or bells, of course, but perhaps with a mechanised hold-all containing mops, brooms, and brushes—to be available on call.

Waggoner had brooded on this problem; he remembered it now, sitting as then, staring down at entwined, knotted knuckles, and, now as then, gritting his teeth (his own remaining bottom teeth grinding against the rather ill-fitting National Health top set); and, now as then, deciding that They had let him down, and his faith in Them had been misplaced.

He had, he now thought with bitterness, been deceived in every assumption he had made. But he had been mistaken, not erring; wrong, not criminal. It was in fact society, just as they said on telly, which had let him down, led him up a garden path which led nowhere.

So he was now following another path, so unmistakeably signposted and marked that no cheating was possible. He had played Their game by Their rules, all his life. Now he would take Their secret bonus.

CHAPTER 11

Mr. Fifterley was dragging again on the lapels of his own robe, pulling downwards as though to bury himself in the courtroom floor or, Waggoner supposed, to establish, to root himself down with a centre of gravity. Since it was now the after-lunch session and Fifterley's face was redder than ever, perhaps it was necessary, he having allowed himself an extra drink or two to bolster flagging spirits. Spirits to support spirits, Waggoner dittied, but realised that there would be no rhyme here, and himself without spirits to make a verse of it.

There was always a sense of unreality about the afternoon proceedings and today they seemed positively dream-like. All the lawyers were standing together below the judge's bench, and the judge himself was leaning over it so that there was a bunch of wigs of varying shades of grey, curls identical, pressed close, twitching as their wearers whispered and nodded.

Waggoner could see that they weren't actually arguing, even if in disagreement; and was confirmed in his suspicion that they were all in it together and that in this play, this charade, they all knew their lines except himself.

However, since he was not required to speak—not allowed to say a word, in fact—and since the part was chosen by himself, it was really all of them, the Learned Gentlemen as they called each other, who were the puppets in Waggoner's play and, though they didn't know it, it was he who had the laugh on them. All that seriousness and pageantry was by his, Waggoner's, own direction. It was he who had brought them here and, though this they didn't know, he who had ordained the end result of all these solemnities! And, after all, Waggoner thought, with the new profundity he had gained through all his tribulations, he was the

People; and in that role it was right that he should dictate: that was the meaning of democracy!

The confabulations over, Fifterley walked his ponderous pace back to his place. The judge allowed his head to droop on its stalk-neck as it had throughout these days, so that, but for the occasional abrupt upward tilt of head, hooded eyes darting, one would have thought he slept. The chief prosecutor was on his feet. His face was red, too, but quite another shade from Fifterley's, with raspberry tones hinting of rich blood beneath thick skin.

It appeared that Fifterley had wanted to take a short cut (to his fee, no doubt) and had tried to get the case stopped before going to the trouble of calling witnesses of his own. The grounds, that Waggoner wasn't fit to stand trial, would have amused Waggoner if he hadn't felt rather annoyed; for, much as he wanted the case finished and done with, he didn't like the idea of being dismissed as a looney—which anyone, he was sure, could tell merely by looking at him that he was not! Apparently the judge agreed with him, and they continued into the soporific afternoon.

When Andy did finally come home, it was still with his leg in plaster up to the thigh, and a pair of crutches he couldn't use.

Waggoner would have thought twice about letting them deliver the old man back in this condition—for after all, who was to look after him? But the matter was out of his hands, since, from cunning or accident, they'd brought him back in the middle of the day, without having warned Waggoner, while he was out at work.

Andy was comfortably installed in bed, having, he gleefully told Waggoner, been carried upstairs by an ambulance man and an ambulance woman. 'Stronger than a man she was, though; like an ox. . . . Never seen such a woman!' He seemed quite pleased with himself as though the giving and accepting of so much trouble conferred some kudos on himself.

'Why'd they put you to bed?' Waggoner was disappointed that

Andy hadn't simply slipped into his former comfortable comforting groove and taken over the household immediately.

'Can't walk, then; can I?' Andy was quite composed, sucking at his pipe. Usually, though Waggoner didn't care for the sounds involved, he found the smell of tobacco pleasant. But now the noises were like those a baby makes placidly drawing on its bottle. It was as though the old man had some inalienable right to lie there, in bed, waiting for food, expecting care rather than dispensing it.

Waggoner stood, reluctant but helpless. 'You want to eat?'

'Well, yes. Do, rather,' Andy nodded. 'Only had me lunch at the hospital; it was early—always is. And it was that white fish they give you.' He pointed the pipe's mouthpiece at Waggoner. 'You know: I'm a sailor. Well, was . . . all me life. Seen fish, eaten fish all the world over. . . . Not that I'm keen on it, but live by the sea live on the sea, so to say. . . . But I never see any fish like that white stuff you get in the hospital.' He shook his head in wonder. 'Only don't know where they get it from. It's like specially *made*.'

But Waggoner was not interested. 'What's for supper, then?'

'I wouldn't know, would I? Only came home this afternoon, and straight up the stairs, not so much as a chance to see into the rooms. . . . All there'd be is what you got in yourself.'

'How long've you got to be in bed? They say?' Waggoner asked with growing apprehension.

'Till me leg supports me,' Andy said, cheerfully enough. 'They tried to teach me to use them crutches, but it was no go. Too heavy, you know? They'll come back and fetch me ten days from now to have the plaster off again. Then they'll tell, they said. . . . O'course, they said that before; and then all was to do over again. Maybe this time it'll be all right.'

'Ten days!' Waggoner was appalled. How was he going to feed and care for the old man? It had been difficult enough to care for himself alone!

'That'll be with luck,' Andy rubbed it in. 'If it's knit together.' He was calm, philosophic, as well he might be. For him, Waggoner reflected gloomily, there were no problems.

Downstairs, he shifted from one side of the dusty shelf to the other the few tins he had accumulated, as though shuffling would produce new and palatable meals. Apart from the inevitable beans, there were several tins of sardines and a rather disproportionate number of processed peas. These, a dozen tins, had been bought in an attempt at efficient housekeeping, Waggoner having found that buying single items wasted effort and time. Unfortunately the peas he had bought, as he found when he opened one tin, were not the luscious pastel pearls, jewelled with dew as pictured on the labels, but tasted like stale bread and were a bright, unnatural green.

There was a loaf of bread, only two days' old, which would do for toast. . . . Sardines on toast! Waggoner had a flash of inspiration. And tea; the old man would hardly have had such an appetising meal in hospital. . . . The cupboard also yielded a packet which, according to the illustration and instructions, would make a delicious and nourishing creamy dessert, tasting of strawberries and cream. But it needed a quantity of milk and Waggoner had forgotten to put out a bottle, so the milkman hadn't left any. So there was only enough left, and that meagrely, for tea, and that was a bit sour. Still, it would have to do. No one had told him the old man was coming home, had they?

Even the preparation of the sardines on toast proved more complex, to need greater powers of generalship, timing, and organization and forethought than one would have thought possible.

One of the pieces of toast was too badly burned to be salvaged by scraping off the charcoaled portion—which meant that there wouldn't be enough for both of them for breakfast. Then, when at last all was ready and the tea made, he faced the problem of how to transport it all upstairs?

Waggoner knew that the household owned a tray, because it had been used in Agnes' time occasionally. When at last he ran it to earth (almost literally), it was actually cobwebbed, having fallen behind the sideboard. By then the sardines, which he put under the grill to keep warm, had become stone-cold again, as he'd forgotten to relight the gas, and had congealed on to the buttered toast as though with adhesive glue.

Tea presented the problem of whether to pour out a cupful—risking slopping it into the saucer—or to transport the complete pot, plus milk bottle. He decided on the first alternative, furtively putting the tray down outside Andy's door to pour back the slops from saucer to cup.

Andy, tranquil against the greying pillow, accepted the tray with a cursory nod of thanks: just as though Waggoner was a nurse, and, fumbling around for knife and fork and finding neither began, unconcerned, to feed himself with morsels sandwich-wise instead.

Waggoner's own meal was no better, but he had the profound joy of being able to prop up his aching feet while he ate, and with the evening's harvest of newspaper tilted against the now-tepid teapot. Afterwards he felt something that resembled hunger but in a strange way more intense and less physical. . . . Food might have assuaged it; but having weighed the relative discomforts of belly and bunions Waggoner stayed where he was, staring moodily at the telly.

Tonight it withheld its customary sedation, all channels leagued to inform, educate, cultivate, or improve. Waggoner, who was in no mood for these, would have liked murder or mayhem; but these were scheduled too late for him. He fiddled with the buttons, going from a discussion of private pension schemes to an earnest panel setting out to prove that there would be no fresh water left on the planet in ten years' time; and then to a mountain-climbing epic he had seen before. Waggoner was not interested in other peoples' pensions; he was upset to hear about the water but expected that They would have something worked out and that, when the time came, he would get his ration. As for climbing mountains, Waggoner regarded this activity with the blank incomprehension of a dog looking in a mirror.

Climbing the stairs to bed was ascent enough; and, come to think of it, the grey-corded risers, with the edges worn bare, were rather reminiscent of the great grim cliff-faces.

He looked in on Andy, who was already asleep although the light was still on: hospital-broken to this unnaturalness. His pipe had slithered from his hand and before going out had smouldered a hole in the bedside rug of white woolly fur, the last Christmas present from Agnes. Waggoner didn't wake the old man, but he was very indignant. The house might have caught fire!

This was another hazard to watch and guard against, yet one more of all the details which were heaping themselves, or being heaped (like the hunchback knapsacks of the mountain-climbers) on his unwilling shoulders. For Waggoner had never asked to take part in this operation. All his life he had not opted out of sports, endeavours, and dangers; he had never thought of opting in, had never contemplated humping burdens, his own or those of others, real or metaphorical.

Once in bed, though tired, he didn't fall asleep at once, beset by the multiplicity of things to remember to do, led on from one necessity to another which was as pressing. He even considered taking some time off from the office till Andy was on his feet again; but the period was too uncertain. A few days wouldn't help and would cost him pay, or annual holiday time.

Untwining himself from the sheets (he hadn't bothered for some time to make the bed properly), Waggoner admonished himself for foolishness. This situation was the opportunity for all the men in rimless spectacles who sat behind the glass barricades of Their various council, welfare, municipal, and social security offices. Now they should be given the chance to show Waggoner what they could do.

They had sent Andy home from hospital to suit Themselves; They must compensate Waggoner for doing part of Their job. There might be something added to Andy's pension, perhaps, for he would need special invalid food, and there might be an allowance for that. . . . Waggoner decided at last to sacrifice one day from work to find out all he could and organise relief. Mr. Hostace wouldn't mind one day; Mr. Hostace might not even know if Waggoner had been there or not. Sometimes Waggoner wondered if Mr. Hostace knew he was ever there?

Still, it was all for the good. Once his affairs were settled he'd be able to concentrate on the job once again. Before his closed eyelids there floated a vision of a white, sturdy pot labelled 'BEEF TEA'; he saw a scrubbed, contented Andy supping from this with a gleaming silver spoon. . . . He wasn't quite sure what beef tea was, but was sure that Andy ought to be having it rather than sardines on burnt toast. He saw the healing potion smilingly served by a white-clad nurse-figure. . . . He knew that once he applied They would see to everything. . . .

Comforted by these expectations he slept at last. But it was a night disturbed by dreams in which he fled wildly, pursued by Miss Hirsh, who even through this headlong scamper, bore triumphantly aloft a tureen of steaming soup. Or he pursued her: it was uncertain which, though both possibilities had that cheating power of dreams, to petrify in flight. Above the perturbation, Andy, face seamed in a smile of lofty and unworldly pleasure, sat, puffing his pipe like a zulu chieftain, clad only in a leopard-skin kaross, and strewing burning embers like benedictory droplets on the rag rug by the kitchen sink.

Waggoner awoke late, and jaundiced. He had forgotten to set the alarm, so had time only to give the old man a cup of tea and the last remaining egg, which boiled to a bullet while he dressed. For the first time in his life he went to the office unshaven and unbreakfasted. He had also forgotten his intention to take the day for settling things.

Miss Hirsh (no longer a figure of nightmare but her normal depressing self) noticed that he was distraught. Despite his forebodings where she was concerned, Waggoner couldn't resist opening his heart.

'They sent the old man home. . . . And he's incapable.'

'Incapable?'

'Of looking after himself. . . . He can't get out of bed, can't even walk yet. And he used to do for me, too,' Waggoner said indignantly.

'They oughtn't have,' Miss Hirsh averred, angry on Waggoner's behalf.

'Only send them home,' Dolores contributed. 'That's all those hospitals want: send them home, get shut of them. My mum . . . well, it was her . . .' She looked sideways at Waggoner. 'It was Serious. An operation. A Big Operation. Stitched all the way up the middle she was after it, like a zip fastener. But they pushed her off home to me dad and me when she couldn't hardly more than sit up.'

'What's one supposed to do?' Waggoner asked in exasperation. 'I can't go on like this. It isn't fair. . . . Not to him nor me, not really.'

'Send 'im back to the hospital, I would,' Dolores suggested.

'They wouldn't take him in.' Waggoner had already thought of that and knew it wouldn't work.

'Go to the Council,' was the best Miss Hirsh could offer; but that was the advice of one who had never met this shadowy entity or come to grips with it. Waggoner, in his first optimistic sallies to get Home Helps, had found that the Council, in all its various guises, was furnished with as many intervoluted and convoluted personae as an octopus has arms, and used them similarly.

Waggoner knew that there were no pat formulas for situations which were, so to speak, not quite pat themselves. But there was plenty to mull over, and the lively discussion was interrupted only by the serving of tea, brought forward a half an hour at Waggoner's request (the biscuit being especially welcome), and by Mr. Hostace, who had become conscious of the nattering outside his office door, which disturbed his concentration on the *Daily Telegraph* crossword puzzle.

But though still without practical counsel, Waggoner went home spiritually comforted, at least, and with knowledge of moral support. Of course his actual situation was no better than before and he really dreaded getting back to the house: that place of former refuge and assuagement from the harassments of the daily round.

Gloomily accepting the fact that the house itself was his main problem, Waggoner found himself at his own door before realising that he had again omitted to buy food; so he had to trudge all the weary way back to the High Street, there to jostle and be jostled by a hornet's nest of women shoppers, all hurriedly buying the ingredients for their husbands' teas.

It was typical of the lack of female foresight, Waggoner thought, that they should leave this to the last moment, forcing people with more important things to do to stand in queues at the paying-out counters, and lifting bubble-plastic trays of eggs from beneath his already outstretched hand, dithering in front of multiple-coloured displays of cornflakes, and, as a final affront, trailing sticky-mouthed children between him and the goods.

Andy had now been home only one day. Waggoner, who already considered that he had been tried in the fires of suffering and could, he hoped, just glimpse beyond them to the pastures of former peace was, if he had only known it, just entering on his calvary.

c.4

CHAPTER 12

The atmosphere in court was unpleasantly humid despite the humming of some machine; and Waggoner realised that outside it must be summer; out there where seasons and weather and unregulated temperatures existed, unchecked by hand of man. He had lost track of the passing seasons, from sheer lack of interest; nor was there any reason why he should take note of their vagaries ever again.

Neither need it bother him that he didn't even know the date. He supposed it must be nearing the end of July, which was Agnes' birthday, though he hadn't needed to remember that, either.

Last year he'd been reminded of it when he'd been clearing out her cupboards and wardrobe. He'd found two of the birthday black handbags, brand new, obviously never used. He supposed that Agnes, with her sensible frugality, was keeping them till the previous gifts were worn out . . . though at that rate she never would have caught up. Together with them had been at least ten of the tiny parcels containing lily of the valley scent, which he always bought her for Christmas. It was always the same scent he bought —as it was the same style of handbag, as near as they had—because it was the one he'd seen on her dressing-table when they were married. Conveniently, too, both scent and handbags could be purchased from the chemist shop next to the station where he got out in the city. Each of the tiny packages had a corner of the wrapping paper torn away; but no more—as though Agnes had just wanted to make sure what was inside them and, having seen (and been pleased with his thoughtfulness, Waggoner assumed), had put it away with the rest of his tokens of dutiful affection.

Of course she could have used the scent and kept the empty bottles as signs and symbols of his devotion. Perhaps it was remotely possible that she no longer liked lily of the valley scent, had disliked it for years and years, and would have preferred another odour, another kind of present altogether, and hadn't wanted to hurt his feelings by telling him so. . . . Waggoner realised that he would never know the truth of this now, and wished he'd thought to ask Agnes . . . though of course he hadn't known about it then, so he couldn't've anyway.

Even without the humidity and the humming he could have worked out that it must be summer now, for then, when his real worst tribulations had begun it was winter: a winter endlessly continuing, it had seemed, constituted of cold, clinkered ashes, a mountain of tins of beans, and a wasteland (despite his better intentions) of stale bread and burnt toast.

'Why,' Mr. Fifterley, Q.C., was now demanding, his voice quivering with patent insincerity, 'why—since, m'lud, motive *must* be proven, must be inherent in the Crown's case: why should my client have done this thing?'

Miming helpless exasperation, he glared at the unresponsive judge, a life-sized doll of horsehair and lamb's wool. His pink and gleaming jowls were directed, with conscious theatricality, from side to side. One would have thought him a man baffled by the sheer unreasonableness of those who had sought to indict his client.

'Why?' he demanded, as though really expecting an answer: 'Why?'

Fifterley continued, doubtless answering his own question, since, as Waggoner had already seen, other people only spoke when addressed, and the lawyers only interrupted each other as part of the performance, parry and stroke, in and out, as in a stately pavane, a performance of strict rules (though these were almost incomprehensible to outsiders), and of doubtful relevance.

It occurred to Waggoner, quite by the way, that Mr. Fifterley's voice was very like Mr. Hostace's. They belonged, he supposed, to the same kind of club, and there Waggoner could imagine Mr. Hostace, centre of attention for his connection with notoriety, talking about him, Waggoner.

'My clerk . . . this chap Waggoner . . .' Waggoner could hear him saying plummily in his plummy club where plum-coloured velvet curtains hung from high ceilings to plum, plush carpets. 'That's my clerk . . . Waggoner!'

The judge must have been considering Fifterley's words, for his rag-doll body was angled towards Waggoner, who sensed the small, cold eyes piercing into him, though they were actually invisible in waxy caverns. Yes, the judge was watching him with the intentness of an entomologist peering at a specimen: not one, necessarily, of any intrinsic rarity or value, but which still had to be classified and adequately categorized, to become a digit in a statistic which would itself be only a detail in a body of such information.

But beneath this impersonal gaze, Waggoner felt, inexplicably, assuaged. Perhaps it was proof of his confidence in the judge and the judge's judgements, trusting that he would dispose of him, Waggoner, where he snugly and correctly belonged; proof, too, of his confidence in Them, in the due processes of the law; and of the ordering of society itself, if it came to that.

Waggoner was sure the judge would know, They would know, that he wasn't a dropout, a flouter of society, an anarchist. The fact was that he was the opposite of all those things. He had placed himself neatly, dropped into his slot, establishing himself in his preordained place in the world, in a society which contained the judge, Mr. Fifterley, Q.C., Mr. Whitely, Q.C., Mr. Nowditch, Dr. Jugend-Phipps, the warders, Miss Hirsh, yes, and Dolores, too, as well as the de-featured faces, unidentified by names, behind the glass barriers, to whom Waggoner had appealed vainly.

In a way Fifterley was speaking the truth because Waggoner, misplaced in this complicated hierarchy, had only been seeking the niche where he belonged. Which was the sort of thing They always said you should do. Find yourself, find your place in society.

. . . Even Waggoner's mother had said the same thing, if in slightly different terms.

Strictly speaking, then, Waggoner really was innocent of wrong-doing!

In the bad winter, the worst winter of his life, his greatest foe, the biggest single inimical feature, had been the Stove.

Some years before her death, when the telly had been as full of advertisements for central heating of all brands as a sandwich is of filling, Agnes had remarked, a shade wistfully, that perhaps they could have storage heating installed. 'It wouldn't cost much.'

Waggoner, shocked, had said the first thing that came into his head. 'It isn't our house! You can't go making improvements like that in someone else's house! Ridiculous, that'd be.'

'You can move the radiators; take them with you if you move,' Agnes had persisted, to his surprise. Because there was no more a question of moving than of spending all that on the house that didn't belong to them. He'd always been quite comfortable as things were, so no more had been said. Agnes it was who, each night and morning, had stoked and raked about a bit and done whatever was necessary to the Stove, which heated the water to blood tempera-ture, kept the kitchen quite snug, and spread pallid warmth to the sitting-room and hall. It even thawed out the rooms upstairs.

Waggoner had paid a quite modest fuel bill each quarter and had never had to think further about the matter. Occasionally he had heard sounds as of distant battle coming from the outhouse by the back door, where the inner parts of the Stove crouched behind a metal door. Once when he'd asked Agnes about this she'd only answered that the Stove was 'acting up.'

'How? What's it do?' Waggoner was politely puzzled, never having encountered the active malignancy of inanimate objects, nor expecting to do so.

But Agnes had merely shrugged without answering directly, so Waggoner had supposed that she hadn't wanted to speak about her own failures; and, after all, household matters were best left to women. Agnes wouldn't have wanted him to interfere, he was sure.

So therefore the thing had continued its existence like some useful but spiteful household beast: a fierce watchdog, perhaps, given to nipping the heels of the family, or a milk-giving goat kept out of nose-range, or a rat-catching cat to which humans are allergic.

Either Andy had inherited from Agnes, or she from him, some skill in ministering to and coaxing this creature, which seemed to have a stubborn, intractable will of its own. So that it was only during Andy's illness, when the winter began and the nights were chill and with water unheated for his weekly bath, that Waggoner had to face the dragon himself.

On the first morning of Andy's absence, when Waggoner turned on, as usual, the tap with the red central plastic knob, from which warm water was wont to flow for his shaving, he was astonished that only cold water came out. He turned it on more, so that water gushed forth like a tidal wave, angry at this break with the pattern of all his years. It took him some minutes, dabbling his finger tips in the icy flood to realise that this phenomenon was connected with the fact that nobody had fed the iron beast below its fuel-fodder. Waggoner knew, but from willing habit had become deaf to the sounds of raking, scraping, clanking, and cloncking which every night and morning came from the nether regions of the house.

That morning, staring at his own face in the mirror, yellow with sour overnight juices not yet dissipated, and its long jaw even more elongated than usual with dire forebodings, Waggoner knew that these sounds, these efforts, these mysterious labours, would now fall on to his own shoulders.

The shoulders, now that he looked at them objectively—as he had not done for years—were narrow and sloping. They were not formed for manual toil such as coal-heaving or stoking. His head (with forehead sloping, too, though in kindness one could call it domed), contained a brain, too fine an instrument to be wasted on the awkward workings of a domestic boiler. His hands with their nicely kept nails were square, but, he considered, shapely, marred only by the bumpiness of the joints, which showed strength. His moustache, which was silky rather than the merely bristly texture of most moustaches, would become contaminated by coal dust. His hair would need more washing, and it was thinning. The barber had warned him that fine hair such as his shouldn't be washed too often.

In the end Waggoner decided he would manage without the stove. The weather was still warm, or could be called warm if one wished to avoid artificial heating. He put on a kettle to heat water for shaving; the public baths were, by a lucky chance, on his way home, though this would need the contrivance of taking soap and towel to the office with him, wrapped in newspaper, which he had to remember to keep from the previous evening.

It was amazing that so much valuable time and energy had to be given to mundane and boring details, which, Waggoner thought, with a rush of self-pity, more fortunate people had managed for them without the slightest effort of their own.

By the time Andy returned to the house a damp and dispiriting autumn had given way to a winter only distinguishable from it by the fact that it was even damper and more dispiriting and by the noticeable shortening of the daylight hours, so that Waggoner left home in the morning and returned in darkness.

The early morning air of the house now positively reeked of what Waggoner supposed must be mildew, or dampness; and he had even noticed a kind of primitive moss growing on his winter shoes when he took them from his wardrobe.

Andy, of course, didn't complain. He had little cause, really, for he was in any case huddled all day beneath his blankets; and when he asked for extra ones Waggoner was able to give him them, since Agnes had no longer any need of hers.

At night, in bed, Waggoner cuddled his feet round the hot-water bottle he had invested in: a man without a wife must have some creature comforts to compensate. Occasionally he thought of Agnes (when the rain slashed against the windows and the wind moaned, cold, cold, and when the fog lay round the house or, beneath a black and crystal sky the stars glinted on ice); he thought of her out there in her own narrow bed, lead-lined—as the undertaker had contracted—and with wood and clay beyond. In spite of her betrayal of him he thought of her without rancour, but with a certain envy, as one who felt neither cold nor hunger, nor the need to deal with either.

When Waggoner did at long last force himself to come to grips with the Stove it was the last straw—or, since the thing was made of solid iron, it would be more appropriate to say the last link—in the chain which had led him to his logical if unorthodox way of solving his problems.

The fuel for the Stove was a kind of artificial coal, called anthracite, and was housed in a large bunker (to which Waggoner had also been blind from years of habitual not-looking), also outside the back door. The boiler opened its maw—or rather, had its maw opened for it with iron claws like those used in some forms of medieval torture—and was fed, shovelful by shovelful, from one aperture to the other.

However, as Waggoner discovered, there was also a process known as raking out, and another, described carefully by Andy, called clinkering, both difficult, tiresome, and requiring skill; otherwise, any step omitted or sketchily done, and the thing either refused to light or, which was worse, having done so, sneakily went out again as soon as Waggoner had gone to bed, so that the mornings greeted him with cold water and rakings and unloadings of the pseudo-coal before the whole process could be done again.

All of this was, of course, ruinous to Waggoner's fingernails, as well as to his temper. He contemplated his hands now. The nails had grown and he had time, plenty of time, really to tend them, filing them to a perfect, rounded shape and pushing back the cuticles. They were quite clean, of course, and his hands were clean too. Cleaner, in fact, than they would have been if normal working life had been taking its daily toll. He had always been rather fussy about personal hygiene.

He had happened to mention this to Dr. Jugend-Phipps, who had given him a straighter look than usual (the doctor usually seemed to look at Waggoner's forehead, as though it was made of glass and he could see the workings of his mind through it); and had interposed one of his rare questions.

Had Waggoner always been as meticulous as he was now, and as particular about cleanliness?

Waggoner had said that, so far as he knew, he hadn't ever been different; he'd always been a clean man. And Jugend-Phipps had added something to the report he seemed to be compiling. But whatever meaning it may have had for the psychiatrist, to be clean, to be able to tend and care for his own person in comfort was one of the pleasures for which Waggoner had bargained away that doubtful asset, freedom.

Mr. Fifterley was just then coming to the grand winding-up, the climax of a peroration. Waggoner hadn't been listening, but the diapason of his voice, the falling inflexions, made it obvious. Waggoner could also hazard a guess that, as was his wont, he had drawn an entirely wrong conclusion, made assumptions the opposite of the truth—and this purposely or because of the total lack of communication between Waggoner and himself: Waggoner was not sure which was the reason.

Therefore it didn't matter, as Nowditch and Fifterley had both stressed to him, that he should not 'speak out.' Perhaps, after all they had been right, and he had better not explain. Because the judge and the jury, like Nowditch and Fifterley, like all the faceless officials in their glass cages, like the warders—friendly or indifferent— like all of Them he had gone to in his trouble: none of them either saw or heard him. They might look at him and they might hear. But they neither saw nor listened to him; not really. Even the doctor (not Jugend-Phipps, the other, the prison doctor, a real doctor, as Waggoner understood it) had prodded and poked and peered down Waggoner's throat and into all his apertures and crevices; but he hadn't ever looked at the complete John Aldous Waggoner. . . .

As though to disprove even this Mr. Fifterley chose that moment to point dramatically at Waggoner: either to stress his remarks or, skilled practitioner that he was, taking advantage of Waggoner's apparently dejected pose. All heads turned towards him, noting the bent head (he was admiring his nails), the thin neck reaching like a dried twig from rumpled collar, attitude pensive, sad, remote.

Waggoner was aware of the stir, like that of so many giant mice appraising a piece of cheese; and also of the impalpable yet unmistakeable sensation of being watched.

With difficulty, he kept a straight face, refrained from staring back at all those blankly curious faces. Since this was a game which must be played he was glad he was being guided through its intricacies so ably. In a way the rules of this law-game, labyrinthine, seemingly there only for obscurity's sake, for the good of the initi- ated, were like those of life itself. For life, too, was lived merely to be existed through; surely there could be no other point?

Since he, Waggoner, had found out this secret, had dredged out this truth from the sludge and mud in which it was buried, then he had done the only thing: to ensure that his own existing was—well, as he wanted it, to suit himself alone. *A la mode* of Waggoner, he thought, and smiled, inwardly, invisibly.

Waggoner's load
Of life *à la mode*
According to code
That's Waggoner's road,
The long, long road . . .

Waggoner hummed this impromptu ditty—(also inwardly, to himself, of course) to the rhythm of a folk ballad, the sort of tune they had in the cowboy epics, so that the last line could be repeated over and over.

Mr. Parsons, the portly warder, detecting this almost subsonic buzzing from the prisoner, leaned forward officiously. But of course at that the sound ceased and Mr. Parsons subsided again, quite without curiosity.

Mr. Fifterley had resumed his seat with an air of accomplishment, in a great flourish of robes and a turning and swaying of torso, a bravura reclining into his seat.

There was a slight accompaniment of sound from the body of the court, as though people had been holding their breaths, perhaps, or merely refraining from coughing and now that the tension was past felt themselves free to do so, scraping the legs of their chairs, rustling papers, and clearing throats.

Apparently the counsel had been making another of his applica- tions to the judge, who, however, had long since turned his eyes from Waggoner and was himself shuffling sheets of paper, as though he hoped to find some answer in their random ordering as the priests of old had done in the scattered entrails of sheep.

Then, when all sounds had ceased, the judge very carefully and with utmost deliberation inserted a finger under his wig at the back, scratched vigorously, and then pushed the papers to one side.

'I must deny your application for dismissal at this stage, Mr. Fifterley,' he said. 'There is a case for your client to answer.'

CHAPTER 13

Waggoner had become mildly interested in the scene, the physical surroundings in which he stood—or rather sat: it was very like watching a telly-play simply because there was nothing better on the other channels. Occasionally one would listen, if only to see how far along they had got.

So that, what with time dragging and then seeming to have taken a great leap forward while he wasn't attending, so to speak, Waggoner was surprised to find that he had been overtaken by a weekend, leaving everything in the case undecided and hanging in the air in most aggravating fashion.

This hiatus, coming when he hadn't expected it, when he'd been hoping for everything to be done with and finished, was decidedly irritating, although, admittedly, he couldn't complain of his treatment.

For the two-day weekend he was kept in the same prison, in the same cell, as during the trial. Apparently they didn't think it worth while to move him. He was decently and quietly kept apart from the other prisoners. It was boring, too, though he admonished himself that he ought really to be relishing the remaining days of his life—for these must certainly be the last two—in which he was John Aldous Waggoner, instead of a number.

The number would be no different from his name and lots of people changed their names from choice: as, again in a sense, Waggoner himself was doing. Those outside would have trouble and expense in making the change. Waggoner wouldn't have to do or spend anything. To do nothing, to be called upon for nothing: this was luxury!

They brought Waggoner newspapers when he asked for them. Leafing through three popular Sundays, he much enjoyed the knowledge that he didn't even have to pay for them. Even in hospital people had to; but not he.

However, his satisfaction with this soon gave way to mild disappointment. He'd had the impression all the time that the papers had for some reason been keeping reports about his case to the barest minimum; and perhaps that was understandable in the case of the dailies while the case was still on. But the Sundays! He would have thought it was just their kind of material. . . . So it was obvious that there must be some policy behind it. Waggoner could only suppose that the papers (which, as every thinking person knew, did as They told them), had been warned off. He supposed that, after all, They wouldn't want everyone to catch on, as he'd done. The whole system would quickly become unworkable altogether if they did!

There was a warder actually in the cell with him nearly the whole time. As Waggoner saw it, They seemed to think he was in need of one as a nanny-guardian fuss-pot, presumably to ensure that he remained sound in mind and limb, to face the due processes of Their laws. Which was nonsense if one thought of the amount of trouble Waggoner had gone to just for that very purpose! But there it was; and Mr. Harris, the friendlier of his two usual companions, sat companionably, engaged in a crossword puzzle, but (shades of Mr. Hostace!) in one of the Sundays which, as everyone knew, was of pretty low standard intellectually.

Waggoner slapped the papers together and put them on his bunk bed. This, though it was made to lift up on to the wall to save space and looked rather plankish, was quite comfortable, really. 'They don't say much. About me,' he remarked.

'Eh?' Mr. Harris regarded him over his spectacles. He didn't seem to have found the crossword easy going in spite of its simplicity.

'About my case,' Waggoner said. 'There isn't much.' He wondered whether Mr. Harris understood Their game. But he thought not. Mr. Harris and all the other Mr. Harrises were too low in the echelons of Their establishment. There was no need for them to know and they weren't bright enough.

'Oh . . .' Mr. Harris ruminated. 'Well, they don't always. You can't tell, really. It depends.'

'But why do they have so much about some cases and hardly anything about others? Like mine?' Waggoner persisted with amused contempt.

Mr. Harris resignedly put his pencil behind his ear, where his skull was recessed as though for this very purpose. 'Why? You want them to write about you? Want your name and picture in the papers?'

His colleague, Mr. Parsons, had opined that this one was as nutty as a fruitcake, whereas he considered that Waggoner was an artful villain who knew exactly what he was about. Mr. Clambers, who'd also had to do with Waggoner, went even further and said that it was a pity they didn't string them up any more like they used to, and that if they did this Waggoner wouldn't have been here, because stringing up was the one thing they didn't like.

Mr. Harris, though agreeing with this proposition as concerning what he called real villains, which was to say professional ones, still considered that Waggoner was undoubtedly a wrong 'un and had known what he was doing all right and ought to be kept away for everybody's good. In this enlightened view he and Waggoner were, had he known it, entirely at one.

'Do I want them to write about me?' Waggoner wondered aloud. 'Well . . . I wouldn't say *want* exactly.' A ray of sunshine was coming in through the window, which, though very small and high up, was not barred. Although the atmosphere of the prison was clean to the point of asepsis yet there were dust motes in the light, dancing like glittering fireflies, dancing round and spiralling up and down, never falling, lighter than the aseptic air; they were suspended, one must suppose forever, like stars in the firmament.

'It's funny, that's all,' Waggoner went on (to see what the simple Mr. Harris would say). 'You know: one always reads a lot in the papers about cases like this.'

'They're more sensational.' Mr. Harris had stopped himself in time from saying that they were more interesting, not wanting to offend Waggoner. Every villain thought his case was going to keep everybody agog. 'The public only wants sensation. And sex,' he added, drawing the pencil from behind his prehensile ear and holding it politely poised.

'Ah!' Waggoner nodded acceptance of this, though of course he knew better. 'Play it down!' he imagined Them saying, speaking with quiet authority into the little desk mikes they used in all the telly business and spy stories. 'Play it cool!' They'd order the reporters, not telling them more than they needed to know. The reporters, naturally, obeyed their bosses.

But: 'Sensation,' he agreed aloud, for the benefit of small-fry Mr. Harris. 'That's right. Sensation and dirt, that's the public. . . . A dirty lot.'

Mr. Harris waited hopefully for more, but none was forthcoming. Waggoner was once again staring at the sunbeam: perhaps, the kindhearted Mr. Harris thought, he was yearning for freedom like any normal person . . . or at least, any normal villain. He sighed. 'What the pot called the kettle,' he muttered.

'Black,' Waggoner supplied absently, 'black.'

'Thanks.' Mr. Harris filled the word in. 'That fits.'

It was strange, ironic, as so much seemed to be these days, that prison was a place of sunlight, symbolised by bright sunbeams, while his home, when he thought about it, appeared always in his memory as encapsulated in dreary and gloomy mists and twilight drizzle. He knew that of course it hadn't been really so; yet it was a fact that the house itself was damp, was becoming damper, and smelt of ultimate decay.

In Agnes' time there hadn't been this musty miasma. She must have kept the cold and mould away, at bay:

> (The cold away,
> The damp at bay, Waggoner rhymed, aside) . . .

kept it all away at bay, with her constant presence, with the warmth of kettles heated on the gas, food cooking in the oven, and, of course, with the obedience of the moloch-bellied Stove.

There had, of course, been summers since she died and there could scarcely have been perpetual dampness and darkness then, though he couldn't remember anything but occasional discomforts such as when excessive heat, solid and heavy as a brass lid clamped down over the sky, had filled the house with flies, apparently come in for shelter; there had been the smell of dustbins in the kitchen and the itching of heavy woollen socks in shoes grown, suddenly, even tighter than usual. Yes, those would have been summer seasons.

The prison, too, was methodically run, as Waggoner had expected. The regime was somewhat Spartan in certain respects, true; but as soon as he was settled he knew he'd be more comfortable. Modern prisons, he knew, were far superior to this one, urban and ancient, where he had to stay for the duration, the enduring of the trial.

It was grey; grey was its predominant colour. But home had become grey too: the grey of dirt, ever increasing and more and more impossible to check or change.

Andy received an occasional visit from the doctor and the district nurse came in quite regularly, he told Waggoner, to look him over and wash him. Every now and then Waggoner himself, from sheer shame, had to change the grey sheets on which the old man lay to clean ones, slightly lighter in colour. This meant that he had then to trek laboriously to the launderette (he felt that he would not have minded quite so much if even the name had been different, less frilly-female); and to sit sullen among the women: the mums with hair in curlers beneath gay gauze scarves and working girls colt-legged in maxis or short-shorts.

Then there was the way home, weighed down with weighty bag along murky streets; Waggoner could hardly bear the squalid martyrdom. He felt each step of the way as a veritable Via Dolorosa; he would be tired and hungry, for once he sat down to eat, to rest his feet and with the telly turned on he knew he couldn't get himself up again.

Andy—when Waggoner dutifully looked in on him, would be lying there, just lying, quite placidly, listening to his little transistor radio. His hands were outside the cover; and they, too, like everything else, had changed colour to the same dirty grey as the sheets, from the robust brown of other days. But they would always be folded calmly together or else holding the little set by its corners, for all the world as though there was nothing else for a pair of hands to do.

Time, which even then had been behaving somewhat erratically, had dragged past. At dreary length the days had built themselves into weeks, into months. The weeks and months had leapfrogged, stealing the slowness of time, so that Waggoner was amazed when, seeing Andy's hands, so changed, so different, he paused to calculate that somehow three months had gone by since the old man's banana-slip.

Three months: two months at home and still he lay in bed. The plaster had been taken off and replaced with bandages; but this was no help to Waggoner, made no material improvement to his way of life. In addition to the nurse there was also a young woman who came several times a week to massage Andy's legs and to try teaching him to stumble round his room on crutches.

Waggoner had never been at home when she came, but the old man enjoyed her visits, and looked forward to them. 'It makes a change, see: a young pretty face,' he told Waggoner, cheerful as always. 'But I'll never learn it. I'm too old and heavy. . . . Can't balance meself. Top-heavy I am.'

'Can't learn . . . but then . . .' Waggoner was too shocked to formulate the thought.

'P'raps later on I might manage with a chair. She showed me: kneeling, pushing meself along, like, back and forth,' Andy said. 'But get around on me own two feet, or with the crutches . . . no.'

Waggoner's mind reeled. He couldn't take in the enormity of this all at once. 'But,' he stammered, 'but, but . . . what about having one of those triangle, no, square things? You push them along: they've got rubber feet. Like kiddy-walkers, or whatever they call them. . . . You know? Wouldn't They give you one of those to walk with?'

'Might.' Andy was doubtful. 'But what's the use? I couldn't manage the stairs on one of them, could I? Let alone go out. But I'm a long way from one of them things yet.'

It struck Waggoner how cool and calm Andy was, how easily he accepted the thought, the knowledge that he might never walk again, never again would be able to go out to the shops, feel the pavements gritty or muddy underfoot or the rain on his face as he moved his head, arms swinging. . . . Never again would he be able to buy the food for the pair of them, get Waggoner's tea, take Waggoner's underwear and sheets and his own to the launderette. . . . Andy didn't seem to care very much at all!

But, tardily pushing his way home through blustery wind on

another grey evening, hugging an armful of bags of ready-made foods, Waggoner admitted that in Andy's place he'd probably take it quite well too. After all it wasn't so bad lying there, waited on, hand and foot!

As always in winter the front door stuck, the wood swollen with damp, and he had to put the shopping down while he struggled with it. He could feel one of the pies crumble in two when he picked it up again. . . . And indoors there was that smell. He had forgotten to stoke the Stove again that morning.

Of course there were no slippers waiting for him in the hall. He directed a bitter smile on himself, at the memory of how he had wished the waiting slippers to have their toes pointing inwards. Now they were upstairs, perhaps where he had kicked them the previous night, beneath the tumble of the unmade and not-to-be-made bed; if he was unlucky they were somewhere else about the house, fallen from weary feet, to be found by chance tomorrow or some other day.

The stairs loomed before him like the face of the mountain the bearded climbers on telly had hauled themselves up—for no reason at all. Waggoner knew that he would have to look in on Andy, for sheer decency's sake before he even set about making their tea.

First he dumped his purchases in the kitchen. The broken pie didn't matter: it would break anyway when you ate it. Waggoner remembered his mother saying that when some piece of food was spoiled or spilt. But one of the eggs had broken too and as though that wasn't bad enough—the price they were—it had stuck itself to a bag of sugar and glued the packet of tea to the carton containing the margarine.

Waggoner frowned at the Stove, shivering. He tried to tell himself that it wasn't so cold, not really. But he knew it was. Suddenly he remembered that there was an old electric radiator in the cupboard under the stairs. They had bought it in a jumble sale at the church for a shilling or two, though Agnes had agreed with him that electric fires were too expensive. But tonight was a time for extravagance, if ever there was one!

He rummaged around and found the thing almost immediately,

where he'd thought it was. It was dusty, but he shook it and the dirt fell off together with flakes of rust. He plugged it in and after a moment or two it filled the kitchen with a stink of tarnished metal as the bars glowed a feeble cherry-red.

> 'Tarnished, varnished,
> Power all harnessed,
> Power unsheathed,
> Warmth unleashed,'

Waggoner muttered, pleased, and not letting himself consider what the electricity would cost. A man must have something!

Andy would be all right upstairs, beneath all those bedclothes; and he'd worry about hot water for the morning later. He couldn't face that monster's black and cindery belly yet.

The old man greeted him with his usual friendly smile: rather complacent, Waggoner was beginning to consider it. The old man really was all right. He was clean—or at least cleanish, for the nurse had been in today: Waggoner could tell by the way the towel was left folded, and Andy's washcloth over the basin, just so.

He threw the evening's garnering of newspapers on the bed, and Andy accepted them with a nod of thanks, but pushed them away with a peevish gesture.

'News. . . . Heard all the news,' he said. The transistor was mewling feebly. 'I'll be needing new batteries tomorrow. These are almost done for.'

'New batteries?' Waggoner was taken aback. 'It was only last week . . . wasn't it? When I brought you some?'

Andy shrugged. 'I lose track of time. Don't know, really. Might have been; but I use it a lot, y'see. Nothing to do else, have I?'

That meant another shop to go into, to wait his turn to be served, not to speak of the money. Waggoner fidgeted round the room, which, nurse or no nurse, smelled musty.

Andy seemed to guess what he was thinking. 'She said—Mrs. Harrison, the nurse, y'know—she said the bed-things want changing. All of them, she said.'

'Who does she think . . . ?' Waggoner began hotly.

'I know, I know, I told her,' Andy pacified. 'I said: "My son-in-law's all alone. He can't do everything. Does too much as it is."'

I thought p'raps she might do something about it herself, see? But she didn't.'

'But what did she say?'

Andy turned up the transistor to its highest pitch, which was now only a tuneless toneless skwark. 'Nothing, really. . . . You know Them. . . . Asked when you'd be retiring, as a matter of fact.'

'What's that her business?'

'Seemed to think you'd be able to see to me better then, that's all. She didn't mean no harm, but o'course they only think of themselves, all of them. . . . Though I can't complain, really, can I?' Andy turned his full attention to the transistor, which was muttering yet another version of the day's news into his large, hairy ear.

That evening, breathing in the fumes of ancient metal-coating, huddled in his chair, trying to digest the tinned meat pudding he'd eaten (an unfortunate choice, since the thing tasted of metal too), Waggoner realised that, far from improving, as he'd always assumed, 'things' were only going to get worse. Everything was on top of him; everything was getting him down.

For once, he set himself deliberately to the act of thinking. The telly was on, of course, but turned to a showing of an old film, which he had the impression he must have seen before—perhaps in his own prime. At any rate the women with curled hair-dos in unbecoming rolls on top of their heads and at the back of their necks, and their flapping skirts and padded shoulders looked like all the others in all the other films, as did the American soldiers: all young, handsome, rather offensively well-fed looking, and always about to punch people on the jaw.

Waggoner had the sound turned down to a growl through which there was only the occasional burst of a bomb or stutter of machine-gun fire.

The nurse had been right. His retirement from Elmwood, Braine & Hostace was only a year or so away. He faced up to it, counted on his fingers: seventeen months to be precise, if they made it as soon as they legally could. And he knew, Mr. Hostace had said himself, hadn't he? that he was only waiting for his own retirement, looking forward to fishing and his garden. . . .

For Waggoner, though, there would be neither. The firm would give him only what he was entitled to, which was next to nothing, and with what They gave you he would have uncomfortably little. Of course there wouldn't be any fares to pay and though, in theory, clothes and keeping up appearances would cost less, Waggoner would hardly be able to spend less than he did now, which was practically nil. He supposed he was not expected to eat so much (being old); and perhaps he might save on more careful shopping. His days would be filled with keeping the house clean and in order, and with Andy.

Looking after Andy would be a full-time though unpaid job in itself. You didn't have to tell Waggoner—he knew—that as soon as he retired there'd be fewer and fewer visits from the nurse; perhaps she'd even stop coming altogether. They might stop bringing in the old man's mid-day meals: he would be expected to see to that himself, for They would know, of course, when he retired. They would have to know, because of his Old Age Pension. He'd have to do something about claiming that, for They didn't turn it on automatically, as They ought, by rights. He might be able to claim some extra shillings on account of Andy; he didn't know, would have to see. So all his spare time would be spent in filling in forms.

So the future with retirement, which meant fishing and flowers to Mr. Hostace, meant drudgery allied to misery to Waggoner. His head reeled already at the thought of the calculations he would have to make: how much money he had represented by the house, the rates, what the old man cost for food, heating . . . There would be hours, days, spent sitting on benches (it always was benches, not chairs, outside the gloomy offices where you came to ask for something), waiting to be interviewed.

Even shopping would take infinitely longer, trudging from shop to shop and counter to counter to see which one had the cheapest fish-fingers or tinned peas. There were always 'special offers,' which you were supposed to buy to save money. Unfortunately they were always things he didn't really need or want: at least not then. And this meant making decisions, weighing up whether it was worth while to buy three packets of floor-washing powder now (intending to wash the floors one day soon and then keep them washed), or wait till he was actually about to use it.

At this point Waggoner decided to stop thinking. It was clearly an unproductive exercise. He creaked wearily to his feet and over to the telly to turn up the sound, though he didn't expect much joy—or even entertainment there. The film was over, though. THE END had floated up over the Statue of Liberty followed by long lists of names and functions, all reeling up to the top of the screen and away, as though taking their places high, high above mortal cares in some filmic heaven.

There was now a discussion of some sort of progress. Respectable, mainly elderly people were seated on a raised platform, or podium, faced by another group on a similar elevation. The two sets of people would be of politely opposing views: as though truth, the solution to the problems of life and death, and the even harder ones of living, could be decided by this verbal tug-of-war. Waggoner knew that these were supposed to represent Us, as opposed to Them. On either side there would nearly always be at least one dark face: African, Jamaican, Indian, or whatever. On one side the white flashing teeth would gleam unnaturally above a clerical collar; on the other from beneath a wild mop of hair. Youth would be there, with uniform of gaudy beads and plastic pants, while Waggoner knew that he was being presented and his views voiced by a middle-aged lady with rigidly waved grey hair and several chins.

Waggoner didn't listen to what they were saying. He had heard variants of it many times before. It was Youth against Age, Black against White, Rich against Poor, or whichever you wanted to identify yourself with. A young-old man with frightened eyes, tugging at a wispy beard beneath his chin, was saying something about 'Viet Na-ahm.' An old-young man, well-barbered and -suited, rallied him rather sharply, with words like 'party-political' and 'sociology.'

But none of them was in any way remotely concerned with Waggoner. A blown-up photo background to the argument showed peasants wearing conical hats and no shoes. But Waggoner didn't sympathise with them, though he knew he was meant to. He wouldn't mind threshing his own rice (if that was what they were doing with the bunches of foliage in their hands); and he was sure that such peasants included neighbouring grandmothers who cared for the ailing Andys among themselves, leaving the breadwinning braves, the Waggoners, to get on with it in peace.

It was the community, it was They, who would have to look after both Andy and him; that was the evening, Waggoner remembered it quite well, when he realised that They simply had to live up to Their responsibilities as the peasants did. One only had to know how to make Them.

CHAPTER 14

There Waggoner had been, sitting woeful and doleful in the cold, metallic air of his own kitchen, with distressful rumblings of a dissatisfied stomach, listening to the young man with the wispy beard and the older man with none, and wishing he could change places with the underprivileged peasants on the backdrop; and now here he was at a bound: warm, fed, cosseted, and about-to-be pigeonholed, in the dock, in the court, and listening to people talking about Waggoner for a change. Waggoner was the subject of their discourse and his fate and future were their concern.

Waggoner really enjoyed the memory of past miseries, now that they were forever past. They heightened his pleasure in the present. He congratulated himself on the vividness of his memory and the way in which he could relive anything he wanted, for contrast or confirmation in his cleverness.

But what was going on at present was not only enjoyable. It was really amusing! Of all people, of all the unlikely people, they had Miss Hirsh up there in the witness-box. Since it was now the turn of Mr. Fifterley to present his (that is to say, Waggoner's) side, she would be speaking for the defence.

She, Miss Hirsh, who had just given her full name as Felicia Patricia Hirsh had come to Waggoner's defence! Waggoner didn't know which was funnier: that she had all these years kept secret the flowery floridity of her name, cloaked beneath her staid lace bosom, or that she should be here at all where surely she had never thought to stand. At least, though, she and the invalid sister would have subject matter for conversation during the rest of their lives!

Mr. Fifterley was using what Waggoner could recognise as his kindly-yet-serious approach. Waggoner had overheard the first few questions.

'No,' Miss Hirsh was saying, 'no, sir. Not his work. No.' She shook her bird's-nest of hair (today crowned with a crunch of ruby velvet shaped like a cow-pat) with added seriousness, with emphasis.

'So it wasn't anything in his work that had obviously changed . . . where you saw a change?'

'No.'

'In what, then, was the change to be seen?' Fifterley was willing words on her as a conjuror sidles a certain card into the hand of his mark.

'Well . . .'

'Yes? Tell us what change you did observe?'

'M'lud!' Mr. Whitely was on his feet, bristling. 'M'lud! The witness has already testified that she saw no change in the accused. Why does my learned friend try to make her now say the opposite?'

There was a pause; then the judge's wig moved fractionally; there was an almost imperceptible spasm of the whey-coloured face. Both lawyers must have gathered some intelligence from these reactions. Mr. Whitely bobbed his wig and sat, obviously satisfied. Fifterley bobbed, too, and then turned his sanguine jowls towards Miss Hirsh again.

'During this time of which you were telling us: the period after his father-in-law, Andrew Matthews, had his accident, and when you saw Waggoner for the last time . . . did you observe any changes, of manner or behaviour?'

Miss Hirsh had received her signal. 'Oh yes. In himself, you mean? Oh yes . . . definitely. Yes.'

'And what were they?' Mr. Fifterley laid down the pencil he had been revolving between his fingers, placing it on the table with an air of achievement.

'Well . . .' Miss Hirsh reflected, eyes like pebbles damp from a receding tide. She jerked her tallowy nose in Waggoner's general direction. 'Well . . . he seemed to get—well, vague. Not that he was Funny, or anything like that. Just vague. You couldn't get him to say nothing—anything, neither.'

'You asked him what was troubling him?'

Mr. Whitely bobbed again and Fifterley swiftly amended. 'You questioned him?'

'Questioned?'

'Did you ask him anything?'

'Well, I did ask him if he was all right, of course. Though you could see,' Miss Hirsh related.

'See?' It was Fifterley at his most silky, sympathetic.

'See that he was—well, that he needed looking after, for one thing. He was untidy. . . . And I didn't think he looked as if he was eating properly.'

'Mr. Fifterley!' the judge piped thinly.

'M'lud!' Fifterley turned again to Miss Hirsh. 'You must not tell us what you assume. Only what you know.'

'Oh! Well, I didn't know anything; not really.'

'What you saw and noted, then?'

'He forgot things,' Miss Hirsh remembered eagerly. 'Very absent-minded he was then.'

'Yes?'

'I remember one day, just about a week before the . . .' Fifterley stopped her with a warning hand upheld. She blinked nervously, showing the whites of her eyes like a scared horse, then resumed bravely. 'Before the—the events. He came in late. In the morning, to the office.'

'That was unusual?'

'Oh yes. I don't know that he'd ever been late before. . . . And he looked whitish; a funny colour. I said: "Whatever's the matter, Mr. Waggoner? You had an accident too?" And he said . . .'

'What did he give you to understand?' purred Mr. Fifterley.

'To understand?' Miss Hirsh seemed about to deny understanding on any level; then understood. 'Oh! That he'd lost his memory. He said . . .'

'No, no. Never mind what he said. . . . As a result of what he told you, what did you do?'

'I told him, I said: "Well," I said, "even if it was only temporary like, you go on home," I said. "Go sick," I said. "Other people do . . ." '

'Go home,' Miss Hirsh had advised solemnly. 'You've got to take these things seriously. See the doctor, I would; he'll give you a note, then you can have a few days off. You need them!'

'A note?' At first Waggoner hadn't quite understood what she meant, because for all his time at Elmwood, Braine & Hostace he'd only stayed away a couple of days at a time, autumn and spring, for one of his Colds. And though he'd filed away reams of certificates from Fogg, Miss Hirsh herself, and the evanescent juniors, he'd never really looked into them.

He sat staring at the gritty window, wondering whether to take her advice; he stabbed with a ball-point at the blotter (redundant now but retained); and that reminded him of his earlier days with the firm, days forever past with all their flavour, when assiduous and anxious office boys filled glass pots with Office Ink, blue and red, smelling like red currants. And the pens, real pens with nibs invitingly gleaming when new, positively luring you to use them; then becoming clogged, rusted, and spluttering until changed by the same anxious but forgetful office boys.

His own loss of memory really had happened, though perhaps he had slightly exaggerated its shattering effect.

It had been that morning. He was preparing breakfast, nowadays reduced, for time-saving, to tea and toast, with the same on a tray for Andy. He was wondering what to prepare for supper, for their tea. The effort of decision at first bewildered and then tortured him. It was a Thursday: begin from there, he told himself. But the knowledge didn't help. Thursday was, of course, by tradition kipper day, and so it would have been in Agnes' days, with the house filled with the comforting, friendly aroma when he came home. . . .

But he reminded himself that neither the grill nor the frying pan had been cleaned; both were caked with rancid fat and would probably poison the kippers if he tried to cook them in either. The Stove, as usual, was out, and so there would be no hot water to clean them. It was all too complicated.

What should he buy, then? Waggoner had learned from experience that, hateful as it was to think of his evening tea while still at breakfast, it was even worse if he didn't and the moment of choice came upon him, weary and unawares, in the supermarket on his way home.

Visions of tins of beans and spaghetti, freezer cabinets of ready-made but costlier goods, banks of cheeses or mysteriously differ-

entiated cuts of bacon swam before his bemused inner eye; superimposed on these was awareness of himself, the shop's wooden
floors grinding his aching feet as he made wrong decisions,
buying incompatible items and then dragging home a shopping
bag which weighed him down and then tore its own handles.

As he became almost frantic with indecision between frozen
fish-fingers or tomatoes and eggs, unable to work out which
would be least difficult to cook, Waggoner suddenly realised that
he needn't make up his mind at that moment, because he was
neither at home deciding nor at the shop buying.

He was, in fact, about to enter the station, though he had
no memory whatsoever of how he had got there, or of anything
between contemplation of his tea-and-toast breakfast (had he con-
sumed it, or not?) and this instant of time. What was he doing at
the station—which he knew was his, though not why he was
there. Where had he been going? And, he asked himself in a
gradual crescendo of panic, why had he been going anywhere?
And who, come to that, was He?

Even now, when it was all safely over, Waggoner could feel
again the lance-like thrust of fear that had seemed to pierce his
spine, sudden and strange, as he asked himself, trying to plot an
identity on a map of shifting paving-stones, on grey passing unknown faces; who am I?

The dismal frontage of the station supplied its own name:
HURLEY GREEN. But it was not his name and it meant
nothing to him, nothing at all. A train was coming slowly to a
grinding halt beyond the station buildings, and the people began
to hurry, jostling him. The train was dark red, but the colour was
overlaid thickly with grey: it was as though the train had inherited
in its train-genes the smoke and steam and dirt of generations of
its progenitors, their outer skins covering its electrically drawn
carriages.

Ought not he, too, be hurrying to get in the train? Waggoner
knew in his shoe soles that he should, but stood rooted by something stronger, more primeval than habit. He had lost himself,
had become a ghost; for in those lost moments he had understood
that the world around existed only if he himself was present in it.

It was, in fact, a projection in the senses of him, of John Waggoner. . . .

He was, of course, John Waggoner. The ground was firm again beneath him, though quivering with the passing of the train, which should have been taking him on his way to the city and his work at Elmwood, Braine & Hostace. He was John Waggoner, long-time clerk and short-term skivvy, widower, and son-in-law. He was also a man who had missed his train and would have to wait nearly half an hour on the wind-teased platform which was open to the cinder-strewn tracks and coal-dusted back yards surrounding it.

The whole experience, if one didn't count the leaving the house and reaching the station, hadn't lasted more than a minute or two. But Waggoner really was shaken. He had suffered a crisis of identity brought on by the need to decide between kippers and sardines . . . Or had it been tomatoes on toast and eggs?

Yes, Waggoner remembered the incident all right, but was slightly surprised that Miss Hirsh had, for he hadn't exaggerated the story in the telling—if anything he'd played it down, for he didn't want them to start thinking he was a bit 'funny.' Waggoner knew that of all the infectious complaints, being 'funny' was the most dangerous. Knowledge of funniness spread faster than one would have thought human word could convey it. Before one knew, there one was, being eyed askance . . .

Waggoner, and doubtless Miss Hirsh likewise, had heard numberless experts explaining with serious faces about mental illness being an illness like any other. But he knew that to the Miss Hirshes of the world (and, truth to tell, also to the Waggoners), whatever the telly-experts said, going potty was going potty, and it was, if not exactly a shame and a disgrace, something to hide, very much like being a drunk . . . even though they said that was an illness too: their faces set in the same concerned yet forgiving expressions as when they discussed taking drugs, or it might be little boys and girls murdering each other.

So Waggoner, after lightening his heart with the telling, had made little of the matter, saying it was a 'dizzy spell,' brought on by being tired. But it seemed that Miss Hirsh had known; and had brought it all out of her lace-covered heart and laid it before Mr. Fifterley, who had decided that it would help him to prove whatever it was he wanted to prove about Waggoner.

He knew Miss Hirsh had been acting from kindness; but it was a pity she couldn't have saved herself the trouble, that he couldn't have told her how unnecessary it was. . . .

The lawyers were muttering among themselves again and the judge dozed, or appeared to do so, and the jurors sat in rather unreal attitudes, like dummies in shop windows. . . . Waggoner tried to remember what he had eventually bought for that evening's meal, and what, if anything, he had cooked for his tea and the old man's.

Right to the end Andy had retained his hearty appetite; and this, for some obscure reason, annoyed, even irritated Waggoner. Because after all, a person who kept to his bed, who had to be waited on, doing nothing towards the general comfort and convenience of the household, at the very least ought to be pernickity and failing in appetite, as weak in eating as in performance.

But Andy ate, cheerfully, whatever Waggoner put before him; if it had been necessary to pamper him, to tempt him to eat in bird-like morsels, Waggoner thought he wouldn't have minded so much. The food had to be carried upstairs on a tray, together with a very large mug of tea, to obviate the need for bringing a second cup. Andy would politely turn off his transistor the moment Waggoner came in with his food, as though preparing himself to listen to words of enlightenment, wisdom, and entertainment. And even when Waggoner was unable to produce more than a cryptic grunt of welcome Andy appeared satisfied: waiting with utmost good humour for words, if they were forthcoming, or for silence if that was to be his lot.

As soon as Waggoner left the room, usually while he was still going down the stairs, he would hear the transistor start up again: but quite softly, so that it didn't disturb him or interfere with the telly when he turned it on a little later.

CHAPTER 15

'Is what you see on the telly important to you? Does what you see affect you? Make you want to do things you wouldn't have thought of?'

That had been the solicitor, Mr. Nowditch, in the course of one of the interviews he'd had with Waggoner quite early on. Somehow, like an untrained dog that has scented a hare but doesn't know in which direction to run, so Nowditch seemed to have scented some kind of telly-orientation in Waggoner. He didn't know—Waggoner conceded that he couldn't be expected to know really—that it was the Box itself which had as good as told him in as many words how to get out of the trap in which he was caught.

Nowditch's appearance was as undistinguished as it is possible for anyone's to be without becoming a recognisable mediocrity. He was seedy to the point of downright shabbiness, which, however, he managed to avoid by a hair's breadth. You would guess that he drank more than was good for him, but it would not occur to you that he drank anything but beer. His no-colour eyes swam like semi-poached eggs in puddles of their own viscosity. These twin yolks now focussed on Waggoner a look which (thanks to the telly, as a matter of fact) he was able to recognise as Searching.

So Waggoner considered carefully how to answer. He had all the time in the world and the Interview Room at the prison was by no means uncomfortable. He could not see that it mattered one way or the other what he said. Nothing that could be said could possibly *matter;* he reminded himself of this yet again.

'Couldn't make any difference, could it?' he therefore responded, though with caution. For Waggoner didn't want Nowditch, or whatever big-wig lawyer Nowditch hired to defend him, to go making out that he'd been influenced. Waggoner wasn't going to be made out a victim if he could help it, someone who had to be told what to think about everything. He'd actually heard nitwits being interviewed on the telly unable to give a straight answer about the weather! Answering every question with another query!

Nowditch gave Waggoner another look, which conveyed—and was patently meant to convey—that he didn't believe Waggoner; who returned his own wide-eyed stare of innocence. After all, he had told Nowditch, said to him in as many words that he was guilty, that he wanted to plead guilty and be punished. That didn't sound like someone doing like they did on the telly, did it? It didn't sound like he was a kind of mindless robot who had to wait to be told, did it?

All the same, if Waggoner had told the whole truth (which he didn't have to, since they weren't going to call him anyway), he would have had to admit that it really had been the telly which, first that night after what he later called his 'black-out,' gave him some insight into what They ought to do for him; and as you might say manured the round. Then, later, there was to come the hint direct . . .

Undoubtedly these questions of Nowditch had given rise to the line Fifterley was to take, and he would have been acting on Nowditch's instructions, if Pekinese can be said to instruct Labrador. And Fifterley, of course, would have been instrumental in calling in Dr. Kurt Jugend-Phipps.

Jugend-Phipps, Waggoner now learned, was a consultant psychiatrist (though what use one who was not for consulting would be he could not imagine); and he had an imposing string of letters after his imposing name. The name itself had either been shaped and hyphenated by himself to suit his personality, or he had by some extraordinary alchemy altered himself to conform to it.

It was early apparent to Waggoner that the judge shared his

own instinctive dislike of the man, and Waggoner would have liked to have told him so. He was by now rather drawn to the judge, on the other hand, and would have been pleased to have his approval. It was a pity that in the nature of things he could not have it, and this was obvious to Waggoner, who—whatever the experts might say—was neither stupid nor crazy.

The judge was now doing his best to embarrass Dr. Jugend-Phipps by pretending not to understand anything he said in answering the questions, doubtless rehearsed between them beforehand, from Fifterley.

'*Homo what?*' he asked.

'*Homo umbilicus.*' Jugend-Phipps sounded perhaps the slightest whit uncertain. Perhaps he had begun to suspect that he was being got at.

The judge looked along the counsels' table, miming wonder. There were a few sycophantic titters. 'And what may that mean?'

'It means umbilical man, your lordship,' Jugend-Phipps submitted.

'Yes. . . . Hrm. I thought it might. . . . I, too, learned Latin. . . . So I would suppose the phrase should, correctly, be *homo umbilicans,* should it not?'

'Er—perhaps. However, it was not invented by me,' Jugend-Phipps said.

'Oh, quite, quite. But my question was: what is the meaning of this phrase which you or your colleagues use? Have you found or described a new genus or sub-species? Does the accused belong to these, if so? Is that what you are trying to tell us?"

'It is a psychological concept, your lordship.'

'Ah! A psychological concept!' The judge bent his wig in his note-writing posture. 'Very well. Please continue.'

'In layman's language,' the doctor said, having his own dig in turn, 'it means that he feels himself utterly dependent: on society in this case. He feels that all his needs are to be satisfied and fed into him from the placenta—society—as a natural phenomenon. He is not one of those, psychopaths or psycho-neuropaths, who want to return to the womb. . . .'

'I should hope not, indeed,' the judge interposed, to renewed titters.

'I speak figuratively, your lordship.' Jugend-Phipps was admirably unruffled still.

'Ah!'

'That is all your finding, after examination?' Fifterley resumed.

'Yes, in brief. That he is a dependent personality, retrograde and clinically insecure and anxious. He has the inadequate personality often found in those who have been institutionalised for long periods.'

Fifterley swayed himself into his closing questions. 'He is what can be called a normal man? You would call him a normal man?'

'No. Definitely not.'

'He cannot be expected to behave normally?'

'Not all the time. . . . No.'

'Abnormal behaviour can be expected from him, then?'

'Yes.'

'That would be when he—with his great degree of dependence —believes it to be called for?'

'Er . . . ?'

Fifterley clarified. 'Behaviour which you or I would consider abnormal can be expected from him; behaviour which he, with his particular character traits, would consider natural?'

'Yes.'

'What we might consider wrong he might think right?'

'Yes. . . . Certainly.'

'Thank you, Dr. Jugend-Phipps. That is all.' Fifterley seated himself with his usual gown-flourish and, probably for the benefit of the jury, managed to look triumphant. Waggoner couldn't see what had really been achieved, besides making him look an idiot, and he was annoyed with Fifterley. But Mr. Whitely for the Crown was getting to his feet. He was going to question Jugend-Phipps and Waggoner could hope that he would be able to make the doctor look the idiot and he himself right in the head.

> Prove I'm not mad
> Or else I'm not bad,

> Because if I'm sane
> I'd do it again,

Waggoner précised for Mr. Whitely's benefit, silently, of course. Anyway, he felt sure he could rely on the prosecutor to prove that he was responsible and sane.

But Mr. Whitely seemed to be having difficulty with the recalcitrant doctor, who didn't seem to want to contradict anything he'd already said. The best he could do was to discomfort him somewhat by trying to force him to describe the norm, from which Waggoner was supposed to differ; and this he was unable to do, obviously not even to his own satisfaction.

He was about to stand down when the judge intervened. 'With your permission,' he bobbed to Mr. Whitely and Mr. Fifterley, who bobbed back at him, 'I think that the jury—like myself— would like to have a few answers, clear and unequivocal, if such is possible in the witness's profession. . . . Hrm!'

Jugend-Phipps cocked a respectfully inclined head towards him.

'Is this man, in your opinion, based on your examination, insane?' the judge asked. A no-nonsense sternness had firmed his voice from whine to croak.

'No.'

'Definitely not? Neither in the use of the word by mere laymen nor in your professional sense?'

'He is definitely not insane, no.' Jugend-Phipps was a trifle more guarded now.

'Is he responsible for his actions?'

There were definite signs of uneasiness. 'The whole point is—the point I was trying to make—is that *his* actions, for which he is responsible—are not, might not be, the same as, with respect, your lordship's . . . or mine.'

'I did ask for clear answers,' the judge complained.

'I can only say that he, er . . . he may act on a set of compulsions which—er—you or I might not have. Which the normal person might not have.' Jugend-Phipps was floundering somewhat, because they had already taught him that 'normal' was a red-flag-to-a-bull word. Still, that was one of his own compulsions.

The judge sighed. 'Are you saying that he hears voices . . . that sort of thing?'

'Oh, no. At least, not that I . . . No. Just that he reasons from premises that other people don't—er, have.'

'He doesn't hear voices, but he does do things you or I wouldn't because he thinks they're right; though you or I would not think so. Does that sum it up?'

'Yes.' Jugend-Phipps was thankful to be off that hook.

'Eccentric, would you call him, then?'

'More—er, than that.'

'More—than—eccentric.' The judge wrote the words with almost insulting deliberation. 'He knows the difference between right and wrong?'

'Er . . .'

'Come, Dr. Jugend-Phipps, surely that is a simple question?'

'No, your lordship.'

'He does not know the difference?'

'I meant: no, it is not a simple question.'

'But perhaps, nonetheless, you can try to give us a short and simple answer?'

'If I had to answer the question with "yes" or "no," I would have to say "no,"' the doctor said slowly. 'But it would not be more than half right. . . . He has his own right and wrong: an ethic which is valid for him. He would not—I *think* he would not do what he considers wrong.'

Strangely enough the judge seemed prepared to accept this, perhaps the least simple answer he had been given. He sat still as though the puppet-master who moved the strings animating his limbs had put down the sticks for a moment. Then the small hand twitched the red velvet cape over the red velvet shoulders. 'One last question, then, if you will be so kind. . . . This man, John Aldous Waggoner: is he or is he not responsible for his actions?'

Jugend-Phipps, too, paused before speaking, as though the answer must be weighed. 'Again: if it must be yes or no . . . I would have to say no. As I said before, *homo umbilicus* . . .'

'Yes, yes, we won't go into all that again. . . . Thank you, Doctor. The man is not, in your opinion, responsible. If there are no further questions from my learned friends . . . ?' The learned friends Fifterley and Whitely bobbed that there were not, and Jugend-Phipps was allowed to tread his thankful way down into the well of the court, there to be lost to Waggoner's view.

CHAPTER 16

Waggoner wasn't at all surprised to see Dr. James in court; in fact he had wondered why he hadn't been called before, by one side or the other. Not, of course that he could add anything relevant; but Waggoner had come to see that this wasn't any criterion. Dr. James had been involved, willy-nilly (it was largely nilly) in the *affaire* Waggoner at several stages. In fact if he had been more involved than he was, Waggoner might not be where he was today.

However, he was not a man to be, or to allow himself to become interested in his patients except insofar as they were walking—or, of course recumbent—sets of symptoms, which he diagnosed if he could, or if not passed on to some higher, or more departmentalised section of his profession. The patients were also, perhaps primarily, an assortment of pieces of paper and cards, on which he kept his eyes fixed for as much of any session with them as possible. It was as though the reality of diseased, aged, or misshapen bodies was distasteful to him and, perhaps, he felt, misleading; while the records and notes were more precise, permanent, and pertinent.

He walked down the court with the peculiar walk Waggoner had noticed before, his toes out-pointed, as though picking his way among ice floes. Fifterley swayed to his feet, giving the doctor that benignant smile with which he graced his own witnesses.

Dr. James listed his credentials, which were, Waggoner considered, rather minimal. He had been Agnes' and his doctor: which was to say that they had presumably been transferred to his 'list' ever since he'd come to the district, replacing the retiring old doctor; and also presumably, at the start of his own professional career, since it wasn't the sort of place anyone with experience or free choice would want to come to.

Waggoner couldn't even have said how long ago that was, how many years ago, since he left all that sort of thing to Agnes and Waggoner hadn't seen the doctor very often.

In fact it was usually just the once or twice a year when he had his flu, which was followed by his catarrh, and Agnes would send him along to the doctor to get something for it. He told her it was 'chronic': in fact one of the only things he could remember with any vividness about his own mother had been of her hawking and whooping every winter. Still, he complied annually, since, after all, it was free.

He had always been sure that the doctor didn't remember him, since he looked at the card every time he needed to use Waggoner's name, which gave him a disembodied feeling; also he had a distrait manner, as though perpetually waiting for the next—and far more important—patient; and this was allied effectively with a briskness which kept each moving, like pieces of unassembled machines on a conveyor belt.

Dr. James was blondish, plumpish, and, Waggoner had always considered, youngish. Now he noticed that the fair curls were, if not actually greying, yet mingled with greyish tendrils. The cherubic cheeks sagged ever so slightly and, as he nervously shifted his shoulders in the witness-box, Waggoner saw that the years of Hurley Green and the generations of its ailing had eroded the youth of Dr. James. Soon they would be calling him the old doctor, as they had his predecessor; and from then it would be only a breath before he took in a fledgling doctor as partner, on whom all the hostility of the patients would be directed while he himself could relax, garnering affection as he had less and less to do with them.

But that day was still far in the future. When Waggoner went to see him, to see what he would do about Andy, he noticed for the first time that the doctor had a very protuberant Adam's apple. Waggoner had always had an extreme, perhaps unreasonable dislike for Adam's apples, particularly for those which moved up and down as their owner spoke, as though the words were being conveyed upwards in a boney lift. Dr. James's was especially prominent and mobile.

However, he was Andy's doctor—since the old man had become part of the Waggoner family unit—and Waggoner felt that it was up to him. Dr. James, who read through the file his nurse-secretary put before him, turned a severe face to Waggoner.

'We've talked about this before!'

'Yes,' Waggoner admitted. He had, in fact, tackled the doctor (briefly and, as he thought, insufficiently) when he'd met him on a Saturday visit to Andy.

'I told you then there's nothing I can do for your father.'

'Father-in-law.'

'Father-in-law, then. . . . I'm not running a social service agency, you know.'

'But . . .'

'Why doesn't your wife look after him if you can't?'

'She's dead,' Waggoner said. 'You gave evidence at the inquest.'

'Ah,' Dr. James said, accepting this as valid excuse; and allowing a silence to develop while he played a five-finger exercise on the papers before him.

'I have to go to work,' Waggoner said at last, defensively. The room was just like the ones in all the telly doctor stories: white-walled, with glass cabinets holding gleaming things, a couch, white-covered, on which Waggoner had never been invited to lie. It was all functional, mysterious, and, like the doctor himself, rejecting. Waggoner felt himself sweating; he hadn't thought of taking off his overcoat. The doctor, master of masterly silences, still said nothing, waiting for Waggoner to go.

'I can't look after him. . . . He's neglected,' Waggoner muttered.

'The nurse? Doesn't the district nurse come? To clean him up and so on?'

'Yes.'

'The social worker; what about the Meals on Wheels?'

'Yes, well . . . But I thought . . . I wanted to put him in a home, where he'd be properly looked after,' Waggoner said, knowing he wasn't doing this well, knowing he wasn't making a case. 'He's alone all day,' he added with forlorn hope.

Dr. James shrugged. 'You could try your luck, of course. But there are plenty a lot worse off, that I know, so I shouldn't think— But that's your business. Anyway, won't you be retiring soon?'

'Couple of years,' Waggoner admitted. He had hesitated to admit it to himself, fighting off the knowledge that retirement would anchor him relentlessly to the kitchen sink and the bedpan.

Waggoner had, as a matter of fact, already spoken to Mr. Hostace. He had told him about Andy, and looked expectantly at him, waiting to hear what he already knew: that, though Elmwood, Braine & Hostace would not object (might perhaps even welcome) his slightly earlier retirement, he could expect nothing from them beyond his legal, skeletal rights.

Mr. Hostace had blinked sympathetically at Waggoner over the rim of his National Health spectacles (which Waggoner recognised because he had the same ones himself) and had sighed, without speaking: a sigh of resignation itself.

The sigh had brought home to Waggoner the fact that Mr. Hostace himself had no hopes for the future: did not expect that the firm would in the foreseeable future, or, indeed, ever, be quoted on the London Stock Exchange, or tycoons fight to take it over. It would go gradually and gently—if not exactly gracefully—downhill, timed to expire with this, the last Mr. Hostace, who, though he had probably not feathered his own nest with ostrich feathers, undoubtedly had it comfortably padded, and kept a pair of privately prescribed and purchased spectacles at home, to wear when he played bridge with his retired stockbroker neighbours. The sigh sealed Waggoner's fate, promising him no more than a certificate, framed in bamboo, acknowledging forty years of faithful service.

Dr. James had forecast it and guessed it. For some reason he has assumed that Waggoner would be resigned to his fate.

'What did you find there, on your arrival that night?' Mr. Fifterley was asking Dr. James, in his most benevolent, cat-like tones.

'I found the—er, the accused,' Dr. James said, unaccountably flustered and ill at ease.

'And what was he doing?'

Dr. James harrumphed into a polite fist. 'Er . . . doing?' His mien was not at all brisk now; perhaps, Waggoner thought, that was a behaviour pattern reserved for patients, to keep them up to the mark.

'The accused. . . . What was he doing when you arrived at the house that night?' Fifterley was at his most urbane.

'Ah, er! He was in a state of hysteria. Hysterical. . . . Shock, I should say.'

'Shock!' One would have supposed that Fifterley received this intelligence with amazement. 'In a state of shock and hysteria,' he emphasised, swaying. 'And what did you do for him?'

'I—er—endeavoured to calm him down,' Dr. James lied.

Waggoner recalled perfectly clearly that the doctor had merely told him, rather curtly, to 'pull himself together' and demanded brusquely to be shown the corpse. He was so indignant that he scrawled the words 'A Lie' on a scrap of paper and tried to catch Fifterley's eyes.

But Fifterley pointedly avoided noticing and after a moment Waggoner realised that there wasn't really any dividend in making out that one of the defence's own witnesses was untrustworthy.

He wasn't quite sure which had annoyed him more: that the doctor had said that he, Waggoner, was hysterical, or that he had said he tried to soothe him. Waggoner knew he had been perfectly calm, and Dr. James had simply turned on his heel and gone upstairs while Waggoner had waited for the police, who should be along any minute; and he was even disinterested enough to consider that somebody ought to complain that they took so long about it.

Waggoner had told them it was murder, had he not? Was murder, then, so common, so ordinary, so routine, that they took it in their measured stride, slowly stepping, constables on the beat? And, surely, even he would hasten his pace at a cry of 'Stop thief'?

The police evidence had already been given, though; and perhaps this had already been explained. Waggoner knew he hadn't been listening very carefully most of the time.

And, anyway, what did it all matter to him? If he were still a citizen, living in the midst of the world's rough hurly-burly, then he might have cause to ask what the police were doing to delay so long. But he was no longer the prospective victim of the plethora of violent crime one saw portrayed every day on telly. . . .

Likewise Dr. James and his evasions; he would never be Dr. James's patient again, and the good doctor could briskly whisk all his patients through his consulting-room like so many dust motes on a dustpan, could brisk them out of life with his no-nonsense wave of the hand, and into their graves with a scrawled signature on one of his proliferating slips of paper . . . for all it mattered to Waggoner.

Without naming Waggoner directly, or the case (because it was still going on, and therefore it was against the rules, so Waggoner was told), one of the newspapers, clearly meaning him, had written that society—which was what They called Themselves —had failed Waggoner.

This, he was convinced, was absolutely true. Waggoner, he himself admitted, was a gentle man: he was opposed to violent action —indeed to any action at all beyond the minimum for maintaining existence. He had given Them every chance, but They had reneged on the promises, explicit or implicit, which They had given him, to keep him in the manner to which he had been accustomed.

For weeks, which had stretched into months, and had, subjectively, elongated into an eternity, he had trudged the Sisyphean rounds of Their offices and bureaux. At first he had done so with definite hopes and plans of how everything could be arranged; but as his demands diminished so did the prospect of any help at all. Then had come desperation.

The offices had all been alike, even in their variations. For instance, all had been clean, yet each had a pungent, individual smell, in which the background ingredient had been ancient, low-grade tobacco; and with this another, which Waggoner identified with brass spittoons, generously filled (though he knew of these only by repute and sight in old Wild West films); and also something akin to damp, wind-driven newsprint.

All had chairs upholstered in shiny plastic, meant to be wiped free of insanitary exudations; in some offices the chairs would be very old, in some new; they would be shabby and comfortable, or new and ill-shaped; yet the family likeness was unmistakeable.

Waggoner would be third, fifth, eighteenth of those waiting: the women with bothersome brats sucking and munching sweets, with shopping bags dangling prefabricated foods through their strings; the men, like himself, mostly carried plastic bags which allowed only transient glimpses of the unmanly contents: detergents, potatoes, and sliced bacon.

People nattered and chattered together, reciting their claims and grievances. But Waggoner kept his to himself. It seemed to him undignified to tell his private business to some stranger who, instead of listening and noting, which would be bad enough, was only waiting for you to draw breath to break in with his own tale of woes.

Then would follow the session in front of the glass partition which separated petitioners from petitioned. These glass barriers were perforated in patterns of small holes, through which the germs on either side could presumably not find their way, while the petitioned were protected against possible missiles, such as eggs, tomatoes or possibly even small homemade bombs, from dissatisfied applicants.

Waggoner confided all into these perforated eardrums; though, of course, different sets of facts according to what he was seeking. When applying (unsuccessfully, as it turned out) for a Home Help, he had to go into great detail, boring and somehow degrading, about his financial status as it was called, which in plain language meant how much money he took home each week. He also explained how difficult it was for him to keep himself neatly and cleanly clothed and reasonably fed. Marital status meant that he was a widower, which explained why he required this free service, which he was sure They were supposed to provide.

His attempt to get Andy taken from the house altogether was quite soon obviously an impossible ambition. It was quickly clear that, to Them, Andy and he (all those rooms, the house to themselves, the two lots of money coming in, the low rent) were very well off in the opinion and on the computerised tabulated lists of the people behind glass.

Everywhere he whispered or shouted, as requested, receiving answers deceptive, remote, from metallic speaking outlets. He then filled in unnumerable questionnaires. Some asked him to write his surname and then his other name, while others wanted the reverse order and all the names he possessed.

Since this was confusing, Waggoner had replies addressed to Mr. Waggoner John, to Mr. Waggoner John Aldous, and so on. All, however varying the forms of address, were unanimous in conveying in different words the fact that They had no intention of doing anything for him.

But as one avenue closed another would appear, dimly, to be open. ('You weren't employed on July 23, 1921, Mr. Waggoner' —'Your wife never paid National Insurance, therefore . . .' or 'Your father-in-law isn't your dependant as defined by section 12(b) a. He's the recipient of the Old Age Pension.') But: 'Go and see the Social Welfare people; they might be able to do something.' Or: 'Try the Superannuated Seamens' Fund' . . .

But the Social Welfare people wanted none of Waggoner, while the Superannuated Seamen turned out to be the Distressed Merchant Seamen, and considered that Andy's only distress was age and sickness, neither of which they could alleviate.

Since it was necessary to visit all these agencies during office hours, when he himself had to take time from his own job at Elmwood, Braine & Hostace, Waggoner was left with little energy or spirit for maintaining the house in even the littered, dust-covered condition to which he had now become used. As though taking the hint from the places where its master spent so much of his time, the house also began cultivating a special evil odour of its own, in which mouse droppings combined with decaying but ante-putrescent garbage.

Andy's room had another, a strong, particular smell, sour and strong, of old man; and this despite the 'blanket baths' administered by the nurse and the pine disinfectant which Waggoner bought and sprayed liberally. This last was like a discordant note in an orchestral diapason in which the underlying, dark motif was mould. And, indeed, opening a long-neglected cupboard where he suspected a broom might be, Waggoner had come upon toadstools (perhaps they were even mushrooms: he could not

distinguish between the species) growing sturdily, even pictur-
esquely in a corner where the wallpaper shone viridian green.

Perhaps the strangest feature of all this period, which in many
ways had an air of the surrealistic, was the fact that Andy himself, the focus of all, the eye of the storm as it were, appeared
not to suffer, and certainly not to deteriorate in any way.

To a large extent he was cared for and buttressed about with
various helper-visitors who brought with them, Waggoner supposed,
some breath of the life outside the bedroom door together with
their services and benefits.

There was also his radio, to which he listened all the time,
so far as Waggoner could tell. Even when he was in the room
with him—which was for as short a period as possible—the
old man now retained the earpiece of the set in the shaggy grey
orifice of his ear; an interested or amused smile would be on
his face and sometimes he would gently sway his head to the
rhythm of some unheard music. Waggoner found himself forced
to keep time with it himself when he spoke or moved in the
room. And this, when he thought about it, was further cause
for annoyance. All his life—he knew and realised—he had been
acting, moving, living, even breathing, to the homophonies of
other people. That he should be doing so now, at second remove,
made it even worse.

He realised that the old man meant no insult; probably he
didn't even realise that he was still listening to the incessant
sound; maybe he thought that the tiny button was invisible.
Certainly he was unaware of hurting.

Andy's flesh though sparse was firm and healthy-looking; his
arms, when the pyjama sleeve fell back to show them, were not
swags of skin hanging from knobbed bone, as with many old
people; they were moulded to tubularity, unmuscled, smooth, like
those of a young girl. His face was a uniform grey-cream, but
even this did not give an impression of unhealthiness: simply
it could be seen that he lived without sun or even shrouded
skies.

But man can live his allotted span, and far more, without
exposure to the sun. And it was becoming increasingly plain to

Waggoner that Andy could go on in this condition of gradual, imperceptible decline for many years to come. He, Waggoner, was now sixty-three. Andy was barely ten years older.

Waggoner watched a fly buzzing angrily round a medicine-bottle from the sweetness of which it had been corked; sweetness of syrup, of glucose, of vitamins, sugar or honey, or a combination of all of these, combined to keep the old man lying here with a smile sweet to match the syrup, contented, a comfortable succubus.

He knew that he couldn't face another week, month, year of this. But the fates could well be menacing him with a decade—or more!

CHAPTER 17

Perhaps it was that same night, perhaps many later—they were all alike—that Waggoner, lying awake, shivering between the icy, frowzy sheets, realised that he had had a Revelation as, he remembered from Sunday school, St. Paul had received on the road to somewhere or other. The actual meaning of the Revelation took a bit of working out and Waggoner wasn't quite sure that it had been deliberately aimed at him (or such as he, for he modestly knew his own insignificance); but that it was world-shaking he did know.

It was very cold in the bedroom but he didn't really notice his discomfort, though the pullover he had donned over his flannel pyjamas had become wedged up round his neck like an outgrown cocoon. He pried out some shreds of tinned stewed steak from between his teeth and scratched vigorously at his feet, which were itchy, perhaps because his socks, retained for warmth, really ought to have been washed a week ago.

That all the clues and answers had been there in the telly-programme Waggoner was sure. He thought of the pictures of the prisoners queuing for their meal in the cafeteria-style restaurant. The food was being served out to them from steaming cauldrons, doled out, dolloped out plentifully, with no mean regard for measure, on to TV-type plates by men (other prisoners, it was said) dressed like chefs, spotlessly attired in white. One couldn't see exactly what they were getting, but it looked good: at least to Waggoner it did.

It certainly compared favourably with any meal Waggoner had had for he didn't know how long. . . . Not since his last holiday at Mrs. Moser's and that had been a year ago, hadn't it?

The tables had been topped with some kind of white shiny

plastic, and there were big plates of cut bread on each so that the men could help themselves in case they were still hungry; also jugs of water and glasses polished, sparkling. The prisoners didn't have to wash up the greasy plates and dishes after their meal. There would be huge machines doing that, automatically, worked by others whose job it was. . . . And there wouldn't be any damp, disgusting, dirty dishcloths or drying-up towels to deal with.

Then they were shown in a big, light room—the common-room they called it, where they had sat watching telly. Some were laughing, chatting together in a group, smoking even. They didn't have to pay any TV licence, did they? Let alone the set itself! And then there were the cells, which were quite pleasant, many with pin-ups on the walls and cupboards while the men were dressed, Waggoner particularly noted, warmly and even smartly, in dark battle-dress type suits which must have been comfortable and like everything else very clean.

Naturally enough the programme wasn't meant as an advertisement for Her Majesty's Prisons. On the contrary, in fact, because it was actually about how bad and appalling prisons really were for their inhabitants. So all these shots were interspersed with snippets of a discussion of the usual kind, among people who were all against prisons. However, this was for different reasons, and none of them interested Waggoner, who could use his eyes, thank you, and saw that what they talked about bore no relation to reality.

He thought once more of the cells. Of course in the dark he couldn't see his own room; but he didn't need to. He knew that the cells, though small, of course, were lighter, cleaner, more convenient, and certainly warmer. The prisoners would have one of those revolts you were always hearing about if they had to put up with the temperature of Waggoner's room, where sometimes, on a cold morning, he could actually see his breath like steam from a kettle! Food, clothes, and lodging, all free; no rent, rates, or taxes, nothing to pay for. Doctors and nurses handy in case you felt a bit under the weather, and even someone to teach you a hobby if you wanted to learn one. . . .

Waggoner's brain worked at it furiously, ranging back and

forth like a hound on a trail: until suddenly, because of the way he was mentally trying to work it out, this way and that, he remembered another telly-programme he'd seen, quite a long while ago. It had been by chance that he'd seen it at all, since he always avoided, almost religiously, all those scientific things. Anything to do with science taxed his brain, Waggoner believed; and he could remember his mother telling him, seeing him bent over a lesson book: 'Don't over-tax your brains. You'll wear them out!'

But before he'd turned it off he'd seen—with an empathy which he hadn't bothered to understand then but did now—a poor little white mouse which was being trained (they called it 'conditioned') as an experiment.

They'd put it into a sort of miniature labyrinth, a thing similar to the cutlery container in the kitchen drawer, but bigger and rather more complex. The idea was that it must learn to negotiate through the only correct set of turnings to the compartment in the middle where there was a piece of cheese.

Again and again the mouse (it was not a very bright one) would bump its pathetic blob of nose and twitching whiskers against the wall of a cul-de-sac: very often the same one, over and over. But having done that, it would eventually learn and choose another turning which, of course, led it into another set of blind alleys from which it also had to extricate itself and find the solitary way leading forward and onwards.

In the end the mouse made it to the centre. They said they wanted to show that it learned more quickly with deterrents (tiny electric shocks every time it touched the barriers) and with cheese in the heart of the maze as reward: things which, Waggoner thought, any fool could have told them without all the paraphernalia.

But it now occurred to him that They weren't wantonly cruel or sadistic. They trained the mouse, not for its benefit, obviously, but so that They could understand the mouse's (and through it Waggoner's) maze-solving abilities.

They had wanted the mouse to find the way through to the cheese; They wanted Waggoner to find his way through, too. And at last he had learned; he had glimpsed the cheesy heart of his troubles. He had stumbled on one of the clues which broke the code.

Had he not seen with his own eyes the comfortable, well-cared-for, well-fed mice-prisoners, contentedly nibbling their perpetually forthcoming daily bread? Just as the mouse, having traversed and rejected blind alleys and cul-de-sacs galore, over and over again, had arrived at its cheese-nirvana in the end?

Of course They couldn't make the clues too easy, or the whole system would break down and there would be more people inside than out. Therefore the conditions of entry had to be rather grim, and were called by all sorts of unattractive names, such as Crime and so on; so that you had to be pretty desperate, really, to take Them up on the offer.

In addition They had put it about pretty widely (it had been said several times on this programme) that those who committed crimes were really ill, not bad; and had been made ill, mentally, of course, by all those who remained outside. And as nobody in their senses wanted to be thought mentally ill, the poor slobs outside did their hard-working best to remain sane and hard-working, in order to support those who, like Waggoner, had seen through the great paradox; or had by luck or chance got into the best free holiday-hotel-sanatorium there had ever been!

But before he slept Waggoner had made up his mind to join that elite inside; he had seen the way and he would trot to the centre of the maze, to spend the rest of his life in eternal peace and perfection in a temperature-controlled haven with nothing to vex him more.

After Waggoner had, as it were, seen the light, he slept soundly, dreaming that all was over and done with and that he was safe and at rest in his mouse-nest haven.

Prevailing over all other sensations was one of warmth: rare and welcome to Waggoner. And all around and enclosing him he could sense rather than feel the protecting shell, the enclosing skin of his bed, which was no longer either restricting, irritating, lumpy, draughty, or evil-smelling. And, somehow, he could also sense the whole world enfolding it and him.

There was his house with inside it his room, his bed, his woolly underwear and socks and pyjamas; and inside these was Waggoner: but a Waggoner grown so insubstantial that he could encompass, his nerve ends could reach out to include everything else—which normally contained him instead.

It was very strange and not at all unpleasant, this all-in-one, one-in-allness; but of course it was only a sort of waking dream, more's the pity, Waggoner told himself, coming very slowly back to the daytime Waggoner as the dirty light of a winter morning sneered through the torn lace curtains (untouched since Agnes had hung them for the last time, crisp, crimped, like fresh-barbered poodles); and he realised that either the alarm clock had stopped or he hadn't bothered to set it. But he didn't want to know what the time was.

Perhaps if he got up now and hurried and went without breakfast he might catch the later train, the 8:35, and not be too disastrously late. But he closed his eyes instead and imagined the office.

Miss Hirsh would raise her scattered eyebrows until they disappeared under her fringe, wondering at his non-appearance. Dolores, digging at her long, silvered fingernails would speculate on disasters befallen him. Fogg would be totally unaware or uncaring whether Waggoner lived or died. Mr. Hostace might or might not know. . . .

No, he couldn't face it, not again. Not ever again. . . . He would phone later and say he was ill, perhaps. It was true, really. He was sick; sick of everything.

> 'I have a chill
> I feel quite ill,
> I need a pill,'

Waggoner murmured dispiritedly, ashamed of the feebleness of the lines. Of course he didn't need any pill, wouldn't take one if he had it. He had had an idea, an inspiration instead.

Lying there, he listened to the muted hum, which would later rise to a muted scream, from the traffic already building up in the High Street, along which the cars raced as though along a track at this time in the morning, with all the conditioned mice pit-pattering along the corridors of the cheese maze.

Waggoner didn't consciously hear this sound as a rule; he had become used to it, though he'd heard them say on telly that decibels could drive you crazy gradually, and affected your nerves. Perhaps the decibels had affected him? He could never remember feeling quite like this before. . . .

It was the sound of civilization, he told himself. It was like that of a scoriatic insect: continuous, without gradations. If you thought about it at all, it reminded you of great wheels turning in a smell of hot oil and ultra-violet light; and words like generator, pylon, power. . . . And stretches of iron-grey pavement peopled with midget-men, for whom, about whom the wheels whined as they went about their button-pushing in concrete bunkers the size of battleships . . .

Waggoner turned over in the warmth he had created himself round himself and slept.

CHAPTER 18

When he did get up Waggoner had eaten breakfast hurriedly, as always, because it was a nuisance; but greedily, because there was this slightly nauseous craving needing to be assuaged with cornflakes and marmalade and tea.

He'd shared out extra-large portions of cornflakes between the two bowls, his and Andy's, emptying the packet since he wouldn't be needing it again, and then pouring over them the remaining milk: there was no sense in keeping it for another day since, to all intents and purposes, there wouldn't be another day.

The condemned man's last breakfast, Waggoner supposed you could call it, though that referred to himself, not Andy. He, poor old man, would be spared further suffering. If he were capable of objective judgement about the matter (which he wasn't), he would be glad—even happy, Waggoner knew.

Seated at the kitchen table among the grisly debris of past meals, Waggoner spooned up his cornflakes, champed at the stale bread and turned on the little, decrepit radio which he kept on the draining-board over the sink now that Agnes wasn't there to get in its way. It crackled out the news, forever new, forever the same. He didn't consciously listen, but the sound was company. The words weren't important for he wasn't called upon for any kind of response. In fact his relationship with the little radio was much the same as he had had with Agnes, he now concluded. . . . Perhaps he ought occasionally to have listened. The radio, when he gave it actual attention, was uttering one of those little homilies which They doubtless provided as spiritual food to carry Waggoner through the day, fortifying the soul while the body is stoking itself with breakfast.

They were talking about some old woman who had died all

alone in her room. The neighbours in the same house hadn't known about it and she was only found some time later, fortuitously. Then, the voice went on, there was on the same day the case of a dog some people had drowned, making sure it died very slowly by tying empty cans to its collar. . . . The moral, which seemed to Waggoner extremely obscure, was that we couldn't call ourselves Christians while such things went on among us.

While both these things seemed very cruel to Waggoner he thought that the people who did that to the dog, meaning it, didn't bother to call themselves anything, obviously; and everyone else, like himself, with the best intentions (even though he didn't like dogs he wouldn't want one harmed unneccessarily), couldn't go around on guard duty to see nobody was hurting one!

But the other case . . . Waggoner had been avoiding thought of it, really, because it was almost as though They had seen clear into Waggoner, and were telling him that he was right; that he, Waggoner, wouldn't leave an old person to die, alone, unloved, and knowing themselves unwanted. It was as though They had divined his decision and told him he was right; and while he was glad to have this confirmed, though he didn't need it, yet he hadn't intended thinking about it at all today. He had other plans.

But surely, he thought (stacking the dirty plates and cups in the sink because it would be a waste to wash them), surely mercy was what Christianity was all about, wasn't it? Weren't They telling Waggoner what he already knew: that he shouldn't agree to anyone, man or dog, being allowed to die, slowly and terribly? And if Waggoner's refusal was what They called being a Christian, well, that was what he'd been thinking himself. Waggoner was going to commit mercy and become a Christian, if he hadn't been one before—which he didn't know, never having thought about it one way or the other.

He put Andy's last breakfast on the tin tray, emptying the remaining half a pot of jam into a dish for the old man to enjoy. He went up the stairs, now able to balance the tray nicely, avoiding the fourth stair where the carpet was worn into a hole, turning himself round like a ballet dancer at the top, then the tray held aloft like a professional waiter would do it, with one hand while the other turned the door handle. He was considering, half seriously, the proposition that there was some kind of telepathic communication through the radio and telly networks, through which he—as everyone who needed it and understood—could receive messages from Them.

There was something simply remembered from childhood about not one swallow (sparrow? robin?) falling, without Them knowing about it. Waggoner had never for a moment thought there was any truth in this, literal or otherwise. It said God, of course; but it meant Them.

'It's just the same.' Waggoner muttered the words more to himself than Andy, propping up the tray on the old man's knees, doing his best to breathe only through his mouth so as not to smell the room's permanent pervading miasma.

Andy raised his eyes, the irises white-mooned, to Waggoner's, mouth already slobbering at the sight and thought of food. In his turn he murmured something that Waggoner didn't catch.

'I'm not going in today,' Waggoner advanced the explanation, not sure whether or not Andy knew it was a weekday and he at home so late.

Andy nodded. Perhaps it was affirmation, agreement, acceptance; or just one more symptom of increasing decrepitude. For as Waggoner went out of the room he looked back and saw the head still nodding, nodding, while the hand patiently manoeuvred the spoon into the moving mouth, as in some kind of parlour game.

He closed the door, then stood outside it, listening, knowing he wouldn't hear anything through the stout old-fashioned wooden door. But he pictured the old man finishing the bowl of cereal, then allowed time for him to chase the last, elusive morsel back and forth around the bowl. Waggoner knew, he could tell to the last instant, how long this process took: he had often watched Andy absorbing nourishment. There was in the sight something of the fascination of waves lapping, hypnotically, uselessly, and with immense prodigality of time, on a shore which they would soon afterwards begin to retreat from again.

When the bowl was empty, Andy would mumble at the bread, dipping it in his tea; then he would slurp up the remaining liquid with powerful suction, tilting the cup till it enveloped his nose (for he could not easily bend his neck any more), and then, all finished, clanking it down on the saucer with loud finality, with satisfaction.

As he stood there, the house seemed to exhale a gust of clammy, stale air round him at that moment: it was as though breathed up through the dark throat of the stair well, from the diseased stomach and bowels of the kitchen and scullery, past the unsavoury cavities of bathroom and lavatory where water had, standing, left layers of calcification or streaks of rust and rings of varicoloured deposits, like geological strata.

The house was a monstrous decaying shell. Behind this door the malignant cell, cause and root of all the decay itself, suffered. . . .

But Waggoner saw that the analogy did not really fit the case. It was not the house he was concerned to save by expunging the malignancy, but himself. He was, he thought, like that 'blithe spirit' in the poem. He couldn't remember any more than that, but he knew that it, like himself, longed for freedom: to be set free.

Shaving—leisurely, for once—Waggoner examined his face in the small circular shaving-glass in the bathroom. (The house was curiously deficient in mirrors, due to Agnes' lack of vanity and Waggoner's own lack of curiosity about his appearance). He could see only sections of himself at a time, but they added up to a sum of him looking quite well, even rested, after such a strange and troubled night.

Perhaps it was the taking of a decision which had relieved him, removed tensions of which he hadn't been aware. Quite suddenly *knowing* what he had to do must be the same sort of feeling a priest had when he finally, irrevocably, made up his mind to take vows. Like Waggoner, he would be giving himself and his future into the hands of a great, all-embracing organization: giving up all responsibility for himself, his cares and problems, body and soul.

Yes, Waggoner would be handing over his soul too. He knew there were clergymen and ministers of all sorts and sects in prison and, though he had never had time for religion in his busy life, he would soon, with all the time in the world at his disposal, be able to shop around, as it were, tasting the various brands (of Christianity, naturally; he did not wish to be thought exotic) and could select at leisure the denomination which suited him best.

Again, it must be a sect not too extreme: nothing which might be termed 'funny,' or call for special diets or clothes. But there should be liberal feast days and holidays to give variety in case he found himself bored by the monotony of prison routine.

Waggoner expected that such a willing—not to say eager—candidate as himself would be eagerly wooed by competing prison chaplains. In the interest of promoting his own congregation, each would be anxious to acquire Waggoner, to add him to his own particular herd of the Saved.

Well, Waggoner thought, he would be fair. He would choose the one which offered not only the most privileges (the frequency of its prison visitors and their generosity), or the most hours of choir practice; but that which he really came to feel had the most —the most relevance for him.

Relevance was an in-word of the present generation, he knew. But perhaps it could still be used by an old fogey like himself. Waggoner grinned tolerantly at his own wetly gleaming, close-shaven reflection. Relevance must have many joys for those with time to explore them; soon he would be one of this happy band.

Just as he was about to leave the house the nurse let herself in with the key left hanging inside the letter box. Her name was Mrs. Harrison, but Waggoner thought of her as Mrs. Harridan because, though he hardly ever saw her, when he did she was always badgering him for something or other, which he was supposed to provide for her ministrations to Andy.

But today she looked at him and merely tutt-tutted.

'I had a bad night; couldn't sleep,' Waggoner lied, trying to slip quickly past her.

'Poor soul! You're worried. No wonder, really. You can't manage,' she comforted.

'I'm late . . . the office,' Waggoner lied once more, for he had no intention of going near the office. As he trotted out he heard her calling after him the things he must get. He shut out the sound of her words as best he could, though 'talcum powder' and 'Vaseline' did get through, jostling their way into his awareness, in spite of himself.

Sheer habit turned him to the station and economy put him on to the train, since he had his season ticket, which it would be a pity not to use. (He wondered whether he might later get a refund for the unused portion.) Somewhere he changed to another line, not really caring where it went but noticing that it was headed, vaguely, 'up west.'

At least not to the office. He thought of it again and knew that he would never be able to enter it, never again could or would gaze upon Miss Hirsh's modesty or Dolores' gummy hair, nor hear, even through the oaken door (hewn by craftsmen for protecting the secrets of their betters in better days), the coughing of Mr. Hostace as he bent over his puzzle. All was abhorrent to him.

And yet the place itself was not really repellent. For some reason the windows of the office came vividly into his mind. The windows of the court, not really similar, except in the fact that Waggoner had never seen either opened, brought back the memory of the memory.

There was a kind of psychic affinity between the two apertures. Behind both Waggoner was and had been confined; through both the sky was to be seen: dirty-grey or smoky, distant blue. But outside the windows of the office, almost at arm's reach (though one could not imagine an arm stretched there), was the wall of another building. It was of brick, drab and time-pocked like an old, sick face, looking as though covered with a web of scum. High up, only to be seen if one stood right by the office windows and looked upwards, a couple of windows in the other building could be dimly made out: they were dark, blind, though an occasional stir of some unknown, unimaginable movement might be seen behind them.

Waggoner wondered why he had never had the curiosity to discover what enterprise, what aspect of life—commercial, charitable, industrial, or perhaps chillingly evil—this wall encapsulated. He did not know whether black masses were celebrated there, or white wedding veils woven. He did not even know to which building in which street the wall, the windows, belonged, not ever having thought about where it lay in relation to the room where he had spent his working life. He had simply lacked the curiosity even to speculate (till now); if he ever had asked, Miss Hirsh would surely have known, naming some prosaic insurance company's branch office, or the British agency for mother-of-pearl workers association. . . . However, not having wondered, never having asked, never having been informed or misinformed (since dark deeds were cloaked), Waggoner was free to speculate as to what lay, what lived, what movement it was that stirred, like some giant, eyeless monster turning in its tank.

Perhaps the place was a way station for the white-slave traffic (if that still existed, was a viable industry in an age of such universal supply). He knew from the telly that behind just such dark and dingy frontages, in just such anonymous warehouses, some remarkably dodgy criminal doings were conducted. Within the great emptiness would be echoes of sound: voices cursing, shots in the night, the thump of huge packing cases into which the female freight could be packed, unconscious if unwilling, and put aboard ships in the nearby docks.

How strange it was that only now, confronted with the other secret (yet not secretive or even remotely evil, window, with its enigmatic yet cosy chimney scene), Waggoner was to think so searchingly about that other; and even that remembered through the fancies—sick fancies, perhaps—of his last ride in the train, when the faceless walls of tunnels and the hollowness of stations out of peak hour had reminded him of that which he had never seen!

The reason for this, Waggoner thought, must be that he had then been in the process of doing that which was now almost complete: relinquishing the responsibility for his own person, so that he could indulge in thoughts and fancies which had been dammed up for so many years. Yes; Waggoner nodded sagely. He must be, fundamentally, a frustrated creative being, tied to the tyranny of the trivial for a lifetime. The train journey, when he had taken himself off, playing truant for the first and last time, had been a foretaste of freedom.

Here, in the court where he could hardly fail, he supposed, to be sentenced for life, the freedom would be made final. Only now, at his advanced age, would he be free to dream, to indulge in fancy and fantasy.

Or so he hoped . . .

A first sudden doubt, the first he had ever had since the grand design had been born, entered into him, squeezed his entrails, his guts, constricting his stomach as though something solid, heavy, and inert had grown there.

Fifterley and the judge were, it seemed, conducting some sort of question and answer session. Fifterley, Waggoner had believed, had shot his bolt: in other words had, with his final, winding-up speech, said all he had to say.

The judge—emerging as he had intermittently before from his role—purely passive, so far as Waggoner could see—was speaking.

'You are submitting that the accused is subnormal, Mr. Fifterley? I would like to get that clear before I embark on my summing-up to the jury.'

The words rustled round the courtroom as though uttered by the desiccated, yellowing pages of a great, leather-bound book, which, given speech, uttered its arid, parched, yet weighty pronouncements. The judge's voice belonged to, and in many ways was similar to the furniture of the place: its stout, oaken benches, worn to the sturdy grain, the heavy panels of the walls and dock and the front of the high-walled throne whereon he sat, scarlet and grey-clad.

'No, m'lud!' Fifterley had lumbered to his feet and stood in his usual attitude, holding himself down by his black silk lapels. 'Not that, exactly. . . . But my submission is that he, not a man of out-standing, or even, perhaps of normal capacity, was utterly influ-enced, indeed at the mercy of what he saw on the television, m'lud.'

'Towards the employment of violence? The commission of crimes? Is that it?' The voice rattled now, like small sticks in a cardboard carton.

'Oh no, m'lud. . . . What I have endeavoured to show, what I think I have brought sufficient evidence to prove, is that the ac-cused does not regard his action as crime, nor himself as a criminal, in any ordinary sense, m'lud. He sees himself as simply apprising himself of his rights.'

'Not . . . crime; not . . . criminal.' The grey wool wig bent over the high counter as the judge evidently wrote down the words. . . . To absolve himself? To absolve Waggoner? To show to some reviewing body that he had grasped Fifterley's point, whether he agreed with it or not? Then the small face was turned yet once again towards Waggoner. The cold light from the window, the matching cold blue-white light of the neons reflected from the judge's rimless spectacles. . . . 'Not crime . . .' It seemed that his lordship needed to chew the words over in order to digest them.

'Very well, Mr. Fifterley,' he said at last.

There had been an unusual stirring and fidgeting in the court over the last few minutes of these exchanges. Waggoner had noticed that there were several more of the reporters, as he supposed they must be, on the press benches. Probably gathered for the kill, come for the final stages, like vultures, he'd told himself. But there had been precious few pickings. . . .

Now, though, they seemed to have found something. He saw that several of them were tiptoeing rapidly away. He wondered why, then understood. They had found their 'story.' There would be headlines that evening:

TELEVISION CRIME!

or perhaps:

THE TELLY TOLD ME, SAYS ACCUSED!

or even:

MURDER BY TELLY?

Waggoner was sure that there would be good, sensible stories about the case at last. Even telly itself would hardly be able to resist the news appeal. There would be interviews, perhaps even this evening, while it was still topical. Waggoner could visualise the suave youngish man, collar-length but well-groomed, shiny hair, in a railway station, perhaps, catching the homegoing commuters, holding out the mike to the unprepared, vacant faces for their verdicts.

'Do you think the television could persuade *you* to commit a crime, sir?'

'Crime? What crime's that?'

'You, madam?' (No time, no seconds to spare for explanations; you knew all about it and had something to say or you didn't). 'What do you think?'

This was an older woman, her head bound with a scarf Russianpeasant-wise. 'Naow! 'Course it don't. . . . The telly . . . don't change nothink, I mean. Can't, can it?'

'You, sir? What do you say? Do you think violence on TV could affect anything you do?'

A young man in a sharply striped suit; perhaps an intelligent comment. 'Me? Affected by telly? We-ow . . . I wouldn't know, would I? I mean, you wouldn't know, would you?'

Or perhaps the interviews might be made among the market-stalls of the Old Kent Road, where people were sharper, shrewder. There would be a schoolteacher: 'The influence can't be disregarded, I mean can it? They see . . . the kids see violence. They think, you know, that's how it's got to be, you know?'

Another woman, younger, trendy, with long, floating hair and huge sunglasses that made her look like a magnified fly. But intelligent, too: 'We-ow: it's relevant, like. Like relevant; see what I mean?'

Relevant? How do you mean?' The interviewer was intelligent, also.

'Relevant: you know. . . . Like themselves, like . . .' (An obvious effort at deep thought.) 'The telly: it's part of their lives. . . . So the violence is too, like. That's how people live, well . . . sort of.'

'And die?'

'We-ow. . . . Yes, I s'pose so. I mean, yes. After all . . .'

In the courtroom there was a strange, intent silence now. Fifterley had seated himself; and it was as though that sound, the actual physical sound of the swish of the silk was significant, a punctuation, a point, a period. Everyone was now listening to the silence created by Fifterley, even the judge, with the last lingering tremolo of his own words swept into the same silence. Even Waggoner, who had not willed to listen to a single word the man had said (but had unavoidably heard quite a few), even Waggoner listened.

It was then that it occurred to Waggoner for the first time that perhaps They didn't want him, to have and to hold forever and ever more. Perhaps They didn't want to keep, support, and succour him for the rest of his natural life, and had freed Themselves, not him, by employment of the devious Fifterley.

Perhaps even, all this was an elaborate ploy, and the decision, the verdict, had already been written; but the game had to be played in the sight of the world, which elected and selected Them. Perhaps all They wanted was to throw him out on to the rubbish heap, leave him to manage as best he could for himself, which meant to rot and fester, to moulder and eventually to die, alone and uncared for. . . .

There was a feeling about all this as though he had seen it all, been through it all before; perhaps he had had his premonitions, though he had never thought them more than anxieties.

Waggoner had ceased to pay attention to the judge, who was now mumbling away, quite inaudibly to Waggoner even if he'd wanted to hear what he was saying. He had turned his doll's body, and was speaking to the jury, not to Waggoner, so it wasn't really his business anyway.

He could hardly wait, though, to get back to his cell. He wanted to be alone, to reassure himself that it would be all right; that, when all was said and done, They couldn't just reject him. And the sooner it was all over and done the better, because then he wouldn't need to bother himself any more.

Waggoner was tired of bothering.

CHAPTER 19

Waggoner got off the train and let himself be wafted upwards in a lift redolent of stale smoke and dirty feet; and wandered out into the day, which belched petrol and diesel fumes into his face. Waggoner remembered the old days, when the city's vapours, like the trains and stations, had smelled of soot and smoke; it had been nicer, really. . . .

The streets were very crowded: much more so than when he had last been in the West End, which must have been quite a long while ago, since he was sure it had been with Agnes. Yes, there were far more people, even though it was mid-morning and you'd expect them to be at work; and they pushed into you more than they used to—or at least it seemed to Waggoner that they did.

The shop windows were lighted up, for the day was dim; they were filled with clothes Waggoner couldn't imagine anyone buying: they all looked as though meant for fancy-dress parties: everything glittering and shining and dangling so you couldn't say what was what, especially with the bright, odd-shaped cut-outs of the window-dressings and signs. After a bit you couldn't hardly distinguish anything, or didn't want to. It was a little like the setting of the telly 'shows,' which Waggoner always suspected were meant to take your attention away from the poor quality of the fare. Perhaps this was done for the same purpose.

The effort to distinguish anything amid so much quickly tired Waggoner. He felt his eyeballs creak with strain, unaccustomed to so many distractions on all sides. His head felt like an empty glass bowl suddenly filled with goldfish. Besides, it was very cold. Oozing slime squelched beneath his shoe soles and the dank air spilled drops, reluctant as the glycerine tears of an ageing actress.

Abruptly, he felt hunger, too. His stomach rumbled and grumbled a loud demand for food. But he was determined never to eat at home again, never to go through the chore of fending for his own meals there. . . . And besides . . . His fingers fumbled out a pound note among the coins in his pocket. He might as well spend it on himself.

Away from the main streets, every pair of door-and-window was another restaurant. Feeling debonaire, not even looking at the menus (the prices) which some displayed, Waggoner entered the first to catch his eye: its window was covered with a lace curtain, which was nice and promised privacy.

Inside the place was dark, so you couldn't tell how far back its recessed alcoves reached. In some of these pairs sat, heads close, talking earnestly or gazing into eyes vis-à-vis. The menu was very large and shiny and Waggoner didn't bother to try to make out what the dishes were: inexplicably the names were in an unknown language. But he saw from the amounts on the right that whatever he had would cost him dear. But money, he reminded himself, was nothing.

So he ordered steak from the waiter with the long, grumpy face (who for some reason was dressed in a blue matador's jacket and tricorn hat) and ate it with appetite when it came, some time later, slightly charcoaled and with gluey lumps in a sauce over it. For his afters he chose something with a fancy name, hoping for a pleasant surprise. But it turned out to be tinned apricots with thin cream poured over them.

So much for high life, Waggoner thought, adding something to the pound note to pay the bill and putting a couple of coins on the waiter's tray for the tip: which he rattled till they jumped like performing fleas. Perhaps the waiter's hand was palsied, like Andy's; perhaps it was contempt. Waggoner didn't care. He wouldn't be passing that way again!

The pace of the people passing along the pavements had quickened. The lights shone brighter in the fading, faded afternoon. Heads were wrapped in scarves, hidden behind umbrellas or bonded in plastic like portions of meat in the supermarket. No faces, no eyes met his directly.

Waggoner walked slowly in spite of the spiteful, spitting dampness. He felt himself invisible. If he were not there at all, feet sloshing in the urban goo of mud, body-shape bearing a film of water on the shoddy of his gabardine winter coat, nobody would ever know. There would remain no record of his passing through the streets, nor in the minds of those he saw but didn't see him.

To all intents and purposes, Waggoner knew that he was no longer really there, in the world of these people, thronging the shops to buy something before thronging home to watch their telly and eat their TV dinners. Waggoner was no longer one of them. He had opted-in, into the elite, which They accepted as Their charges.

Purposefully, Waggoner turned into the Underground. With a delicious sense of extravagance he went to the newspaper kiosk and, deliberately, enjoying every moment, bought himself an evening paper. Pristine, its uncrumpled folds smooth as fresh-ironed linen, he held it tenderly against his body, under his arm. He would read it later, he supposed. But whether he got full value of it or not didn't matter; the money he was spending now was Their money, since surely everything would be taken from him.

It was compounding pleasure to spend Their money on a luxury he had never allowed himself.

Treading the streets back to Pontefract Crescent, Waggoner tried to give himself the full thrill of finality, realising, knowing right down to his aching shoe soles that this was the last time he would pass them by.

But his flesh, his spirit had lost the skill of excitement; his mind knew that this was epochal, but nothing happened. His heart beat no faster, the blood ran no more freely or hotly; there were tears in his eyes, but they were the normal ones brought about by the chilly wind and meant nothing. They did not even feel warm on his cheeks.

> The last time past
> This bally alley,
> Never again
> Edge Hill in rain,

he told himself. But neither the poem nor any emotion stirred him. Once more up Blenheim Rise and he could look along the hundred-yard length of Balaclava, the cul-de-sac. Then up again the length of Bannockburn Hill, whose stones he knew he would never press again, and into Pontefract Crescent; but the stones were no more moved than he.

The slate-blue roofs were slimy with rain, the spiked peaks pointing contemptuously to the sky. The privet hedges concealed the miniature front gardens: tidy, neglected, or shrubby—the hedges hid them all. In some porches perambulators huddled forlornly; motorcycles shrouded in tarpaulins in others. Rain made coloured snail-track patterns where oil had been spilt in the roads.

And here, too, the few people he passed seemed to take less notice of Waggoner than did the privets or the empty windows.

It was the last time, but it could have been the first, or the thousandth. The streets he passed through were closing up after Waggoner like the pages of a book that has been read. As far as Waggoner was concerned (which was to say effectively), they would henceforth cease to exist.

It was a day, an evening for ceasing.

The trial had now been going on for a number of days; it was drawing to a dreary and quite predictable close. Once more, after the brief flurry of excitement (which had not produced a great deal in the way even of minor headlines), the press benches gaped empty like a mouth of decayed teeth. A few depressed juniors held the fort against the unlikely event of the newsworthy event. There were other courts trying livelier, more up-to-date crimes and criminals: some protagonists were young or wildly enough dressed to be called pop singers or starlets, for newspaper purposes, or were important enough as smugglers of minks or jewels or art treasures to become instant jet-setters, trend-setters.

Waggoner knew that he could never be included in any of these categories. His life-style (for he knew the words, even if he never had occasion to use them) was too mundane. Therefore he tried not to feel hurt by the neglect. And since he had, in effect, retired from the world, it ought not to matter to him if the world treated him to its ephemeral curiosity or not.

But in the world or apart from it he was still a human being, wasn't he? A human being, moreover, in a dramatic, traumatic, climactic situation! If he could speak to a telly-interviewer now, he would simply ask him: 'Am I a human being or not?' The answer would have to be 'Yes!' So why, then, were the purveyors of popular publicity ignoring him?

Well, he should care! It wouldn't put anything in his purse or pocket however many columns they wrote about him. The neat, battle-dress type suit they would give him would only have one pocket, he expected. It would be enough for him!

He knew that most prisoners kept their tobacco (they called it 'snout') in this pocket. But Waggoner, who had never smoked, had no intention of starting now, even though it would be free. He could change his share for something else—sweets, perhaps, or extra jam.

Come to that, he didn't even need one pocket! His mother had shown him how to keep his handkerchief stuffed up his coat sleeve like a gentleman; it had been a habit of lifelong usefulness and convenience, and he was grateful to her for the advice. And he wouldn't have to carry keys, tickets, pencils, money . . . or indeed anything else!

Well, this comfort of not-needing was his right; and he had sought it with industry and patience just as the mouse had had to in its more overt labyrinth. It was like the game of Hunt the Slipper: it had been passed always from one bureaucratic hand to another. . . . Yes, the slipper was as good a symbol as could be of what he had been hunting through the maze. *'Slippered ease,'* Waggoner remembered, was a quotation from some poem or other he'd learned at school.

He'd been quite good at 'learning by heart' as English literature was then taught. Some tags and bits, ragged as ancient banners, fluttered still among the darkling rafters of his memory. There was *'Stern daughter of the voice of God,'* for instance: it was duty they meant, he thought. And no one could say that Waggoner hadn't done his duty, right to the end.

The judge was making a long speech.

Fifterley and Mr. Whiting, the opposition, were both leaning back in their chairs, listening, Waggoner supposed. But not he! In any case the judge was speaking to the jury, that collection of cardboard figures, some of whom now, for the first time in so many days, were actually looking at him, Waggoner thought. And so for the first time, with awakening curiosity, he looked at them.

Spectacles in dark frames and rimless ones with gold earpieces were turned in his direction, lighted little round windows looking into his soul. There were beetling brows, caverned hollows, and the blue, protuberant eyes of the buxom lady who was the only one Waggoner had noticed before, because she was so like the woman in the cocoa commercial—very like indeed. Her eyes were surprised; but Waggoner, looking closely, realised that this was on account of her having plucked her eyebrows in high, round curves. She would not be surprised at all: unless, perhaps, Waggoner were to tell her the recipe for Toad-in-the-Hole, which was the last thing he had heard on Andy's little radio. . . . But then, come to think of it, that would be the sort of thing she would know already.

Perhaps he ought really to have examined the jury more carefully and closely before. It would not have altered his own fate in any way, of course; but it might have been more interesting if he'd spent some time speculating about them instead of losing himself in the rather fruitless and chaotic memories of past days. Because these people were really Them personified.

Waggoner realised that he had been mistaken in taking for granted the fact that the judge and Mr. Fifterley, Q.C., and Mr. Whiting, Q.C., were the particular tentacle of Them which held him. The judge, like the lawyers, were there to tell the jury, the real Them how to carry out the laws which They had made, and all of them together and the warders and the clerks of the court and the policemen, yes, and Waggoner himself, were all there to play the game by Their rules.

It was a change of viewpoint rather than another revelation. And, unfortunately, even seen as it were in the flesh, in the round, the jury were still an uninspiring lot—again, typical, Waggoner supposed.

Apart from the cocoa-lady there was only one other woman: slight, rather well-dressed, neither old nor young, and with the look, he thought, of a teacher at a 'good' school. Somehow one knew that she was unmarried, and that she would make wry jokes about her own spinsterhood to hide the fact that she minded. . . . Next to her was a man of indefinable middle-age with a face smooth as though carved from salmon-pink plastic. A rectangular white moustache, short-cropped, was centred precisely beneath his nose and he wore a bow tie. He sat very upright; and he had been wearing a bow tie every day, Waggoner now recalled. . . . He was also now aware of a deep-seated distrust, even suspicion, of bow-tie wearers; or rather of the sort of people they must be. The man also had a square head of neat white stubble and straight-aligned eyes, fixed unswervingly on Waggoner.

Made uneasy by this scrutiny, Waggoner let his own gaze pass with self-conscious *sang-froid* across the remaining faces. But there were really none worth closer examination. One man he thought, was coloured: perhaps a Jamaican, and Waggoner wondered whether it was right for them to let a foreigner sit to decide about a born Britisher like himself. Another of them must, he was sure, be too young. . . . Neither of those two, the foreigner nor the almost-youth, could possibly understand the situation of a man of Waggoner's age and experience: a man who, if he had been judged fit, might have fought in the war for the Old Country: before either of them were in it!

But still, they were all rubber stamps, really. The judge was still telling them what to say, or so it sounded to Waggoner, though he knew the judge wasn't supposed to. At the moment he was saying something unnecessarily rude about Waggoner's mental condition, which, Waggoner would have liked to wager, was as good as his own!

Only he found it mildly troubling that they all continued to watch him, though at the same time you could tell they were listening to the old judge.

It was exactly as though a class of students was examining a specimen—botanical or animal—while the lecturer explained its peculiarities. Sometimes on the telly there would be a programme (seen accidentally or from ennui by Waggoner) in which a machine or some other quite incomprehensible scientific thing was shown, while a voice, with the thinnest possible veneer of condescension, accompanied the close-ups and the vastly magnified pictures of the thing.

Waggoner felt himself just such an object as the coolly appraising eyes were bent on him rather than—as would be more natural, you would think—on the source of the voice.

Fifterley continued with satisfied mien. Waggoner would not have been at all surprised—indeed, it now seemed quite feasible—that he and Whiting and the judge had all put their wigs together (as Waggoner had seen them doing in fact) and had decided it all from the beginning. They would have known from experience what would influence the jurors, knowing Them, being, really, the power behind Them. . . .

Unreasonably and unaware of what he was doing, Waggoner had allowed strain to make his neck muscles rigid, to dry his eyes in their sockets, and to make him tremble with tension in his extremities.

His mouth was dry too; he leaned forward and took a sip of water from the glass which reposed on a ledge of the dock, down out of view of the public. The water tasted of dust and, faintly, of disinfectant.

Waggoner chided himself for being a silly-billy. It was his mother's phrase (for some reason she was more in his mind these days than in all the years put together since he'd seen her for the casual last time); she had used it to mean fussing without cause, getting upset about nothing. The words, the message came into his head as from a distant star.

All was well; nothing could go wrong ever again. They knew what was best for Waggoner; and he himself had understood it in time.

The future, which, like the water, would have a faint bouquet of disinfectant, beckoned to Waggoner: its white-tiled corridors, its orderly Quiet Rooms, its noisy and jolly telly rooms, its monotonous but unfailing fare—all these were waiting to enfold and protect him for the rest of his life.

Waggoner sighed with a foretaste of contentment and resumed not listening.

CHAPTER 20

The jury filed out.

Always before they had been already seated when Waggoner came into the court and left it only after he himself had gone, so that they had been a kind of living background, a human wallpapering to everything else. So that Waggoner was taken aback when he saw them, people, individuals, get to their feet and walk.

There were surprises: the man with the beetling brows, who looked so burly and commanding, turned out to be a short fellow, waddling in an undignified fashion, who could scarcely have commanded a bus at a request stop. Waggoner's favourite, the motherly cocoa-lady, hugged a modish spotted leopard-like coat up around her and gold linted from her wrists. She no longer looked a neighbouring homebody, and Waggoner was disconcerted, as anyone would be who, believing himself to be confronted with a particular group of people, suddenly finds them to be completely different.

He was still bewildered when he himself was shepherded from the dock, down the dark, wood-panelled spiral stairs, so that he stumbled and might even have fallen if Mr. Parsons had not grabbed him by the arm, while Mr. Harris following on said 'Steady!' in a friendly voice.

Waggoner nodded. Of course he would be steady. It was only the surprise, and darkness suddenly after the lighted court. He would be steady. This, after all, would be the last day.

They sat him in a small room—a cell it must be really, he supposed—and brought him a cup of the inevitable tea. It was hot and strong and sweet and Waggoner enjoyed it, feeling new life uncoiling inside him.

He didn't think of much, sitting there, because there wasn't even a newspaper, which was not very thoughtful of Them. Andy did come into his mind in a vague kind of way, since all of this was really about Andy, though in the cumbersome processes of the law the old man had become even more of a cipher than Waggoner himself. . . .

When he'd entered Andy's room after his day out, the day of his truancy, the old man was leaning back against his pillows. He seemed drowsy, probably with repletion, because the Meals on Wheels tray was pushed to the foot of the bed, trailing gravy and custard among the blotchy blankets. Beneath his fingers, clutched by black-rimmed nails, was the transistor, as usual.

A woman's voice was bleating with cheerful cheeriness: 'Why don't you give your husband a pleasant surprise tonight, and serve his sausages in this *new* way, which is really an *old* one, and it's so easy and delicious. . . .' Waggoner paused for a moment, hand on the instrument. What was this new way which was also old? He might as well hear.

'It's called Toad-in-the-Hole,' the voice continued warmly, 'and it's appetising and sustaining too. First take your sausages: of course how many will depend on how many people you're serving. . . .'

Waggoner saw that Andy's eyes were now open and that he was looking at him: enquiringly, he thought. Waggoner nodded yes, though to what question he did not know. He reached down for the transistor, but the old man held on, unwilling to release it, and Waggoner had to unbend the fingers, one by one.

'Sift the flour and add a half a teaspoonful of salt,' the woman's voice said, as he very gently lifted Andy's head from the pillow and then pressed it down, hard, over his face, over the still questioning open eyes, the mouth gaping with surprise in the last instant, and shutting out, blotting out the whole of the rest of their lives from that moment forward.

Waggoner was distressed that Andy's limbs, which had seemed so weak and twig-like, squirmed and thrashed about for what seemed a long time with a great deal of force; but it couldn't have lasted more than a minute or two, for, as he pressed down harder than ever and the twitching stopped, the recipe had not even entered the oven stage.

'The batter should be thick and creamy, but be careful there aren't any lumps; and then pour it over the sausages. It may not cover them completely. . . .'

Waggoner reached out and turned the radio off; after all, he wouldn't be doing any cooking any more. He left the pillow where it was; he didn't want to see Andy's face and anyway he knew one shouldn't touch a corpse until the police came to see it.

He'd left a sixpence handy on the hall table. . . . He hadn't even taken off his coat, so he went straight outside again and down the street to the phone box. Only there, ringing 999, did he realise that you didn't need sixpence for that. So he decided that he might as well ring the doctor too. . . .

When a voice answered the 999 call almost immediately, 'Police,' Waggoner said, 'I want the police. . . .'

In the event Dr. James had come before the police, and had gone upstairs to Andy as calmly as though Waggoner had said the old man had flu.

Waggoner, still watching for the police from the front-window, was disappointed a little that when they did drive up it wasn't at all like telly. There was no siren, not even their blue lamp on top of the car alight. . . .

For some reason the next while was a bit hazy in his mind: mixed up, really, what actually happened (which was appallingly anti-climactic) with the layers of questions and answers and evidence about it that had come so much later. Waggoner couldn't have said for sure just what the police did and said, or in what order.

There were only two of them and they seemed astonishingly unconcerned, until Waggoner realised that they hadn't known what to expect, even though he'd told them on the phone.

But even afterwards, after he'd taken them upstairs to see Andy and he'd assured them again that he'd meant to do it, that it wasn't any accident, and Dr. James had given them all a funny look and refused to say anything, even then they'd taken it far more calmly than he'd expected.

They didn't, for instance, clap handcuffs on him, or even loom over him menacingly. He could, for that matter, have walked away, through the back door and out and off if he'd wanted, while one of them was phoning from his car and the other doing whatever it was he wanted to do upstairs. Even when they left the house he didn't have a coat over his head, wasn't wrapped in a blanket not to be recognised like the suspects he'd always seen in the news.

There were a lot of car journeys after that, interspersed with various people talking to him; but all did so quite kindly, even disappointingly so. He really couldn't remember who said what to him, not even to oblige Mr. Fifterley, who had tried so hard to make him, so that he could be seen to be earning his fee.

But Waggoner wasn't going to over-tax his brains for him; not he, especially not now, when he was in sight of the white-tiled peaceful haven where the only thinking he would have to do was to choose between tea or cocoa (perhaps not even that); or on which radio programme he would have his earphones plugged. . . .

Waggoner wasn't even sure the old man had known his dying for what it was; there had been no suffering. There might have been a few unpleasant moments but they had been quickly over. There could hardly have been panic, he didn't think. . . . He wouldn't have wanted anything unpleasant for Andy. In the last year Waggoner had become quite fond of the old man; or perhaps it would be more exact to say that he'd become used to him. And yet in that same period he had come to hate the old man's body because it was such an insufferable nuisance to both of them. Andy himself must have been as glad to be rid of the burden of it as was Waggoner—or would have been if he'd known and could have chosen.

On his last visit the doctor had said with macabre cheerfulness to the living Andy that he was strong and healthy, and could live many years: 'You'll see a hundred yet,' he'd said, winking at Waggoner aside to imply that, if not a hundred, the old man might outlive them both. . . .

And yet he had put up only the slightest resistance. Had he known what Waggoner was doing and been grateful? Had he known?

Waggoner cast a doubtful glance up at the dingy grey ceiling. He had never believed—not to say really believed—in life after death, and he couldn't believe that Andy was there above, suspended in a hazy heaven above the sky. After all, the astronauts had been pretty high, hadn't they, and found nothing except the moon, which had been exactly where they had known it would be? And there were maps of the skies showing nothing but stars and then more stars, endlessly. The skies went all around, so heaven and hell, if they were anywhere, would have to be both up and down, above and below. No, there was no sense in it at all.

Andy was dead and that was the end of him. That one day there would be no more Waggoner must also, logically, be certain; though, since he couldn't imagine it, perhaps it was not so. After all, when he ceased to be, there wouldn't be anything else, would there? Without him to see it?

Perhaps it was on purpose that they'd not even given him a newspaper. Perhaps he was supposed to think, to brood. Perhaps they wanted him to worry? Well, he was worrying, wasn't he? Thinking and worrying were the same, really. . . .

So it was lucky that, as the clock on the wall showed, it wasn't much above half an hour before they came for him and told him the jury was in again.

Which was long enough, really, seeing that the judge had told them what to say, though Mr. Parsons muttered that it was quick, like.

Blinking in the light of the court, which always seemed brighter than it really was after the dark stairs, Waggoner listened to a whole meaningless rigmarole. In a way it was still part of the sort of set-piece stuff They went in for, like the judge's black cap used to be in the old days, the bad old days, when They sentenced you to death.

The foreman of the jury was standing up (it was the white-moustached man, as you would expect) and the clerk was asking him questions.

Waggoner didn't understand at first when the man said that they found him Not Guilty. Not until the judge turned his small insect-face to him: 'John Aldous Waggoner!'

There was a sharp poke in the small of his back from Mr. Parsons, and Waggoner didn't know at first what was expected of him, since he was already on his feet (never having sat down, in fact). Still, he did his best and turned his whole body, at attention, to the judge, and gripped the brass rail of the front of the dock. It was cold in his hands. . . .

By the time he was ready to take it in, it was all over. 'By reason of diminished responsibility,' the judge was telling him—whatever that meant. And Mr. Parsons was giving him another poke in the back, and the small door, which he had never noticed before, in the side of the dock was opened, and he stepped down on to the floor of the court.

From here everything looked strange, a different perspective, the geography changed. The only familiar landmark was Mr. Fifterley, who was gathering up his papers, oblivious of him as though he had never heard of Waggoner.

Waggoner hastened to intercept him, his guide through the wilderness. 'What does it mean?' he asked.

'Mean?' Fifterley snapped closed the clasps of his briefcase. 'Means you're free. Free as air.'

'Free?'

'Innocent,' Fifterley said. 'You can just go. That's all.'

'Innocent,' Waggoner repeated. He felt his eyes gel like dead fishes'. 'How . . . What does it mean? This "diminished responsibility"?'

'That you're innocent. . . . You didn't know what you were doing. Therefore you're innocent. . . .' He leaned his red, golf-playing face close to Waggoner, wafting a scent of eau de cologne and mouthwash. 'It means, my friend,' said Fifterley, 'that you've committed the perfect murder. . . . And if you ever say I said so, I'll say you're a liar as well!'

He turned on his well-heeled heel and left Waggoner standing there, a free man. He still didn't know what to make of it, except that They had rejected him and would not take him into Their enfolding haven.

CHAPTER 21

The house still, after all this time, smelt faintly of Andy—or perhaps it was Waggoner's imagination that supplied the whiff of sour old-man smell superimposed on that of mouse droppings and mouldiness.

His slippers, he saw, were huddled together as though ashamed by the wall at the bottom of the stairs. As he toed them, old friends, they fell apart, showing dirt-grey fungus. He would have to buy another pair—if he could.

He turned the money, the coins in his pocket; he knew them well, old acquaintances that had been taken from him at the police station and were now returned. Sixty-two and a half new pence: the sum written on a receipt, signed by the prison officer. It had seemed a trivial and paltry sum then; now it had larger areas of need to cover. New slippers, for instance.

On the mat beneath the letter box were several envelopes. Advertisements . . . for things he didn't want, couldn't have if he did. But one was a business envelope, a real letter. Waggoner took it to the front door, positioned it beneath the orange segment of glass, and opened it.

The lettered heading of Elmwood, Braine & Hostace was so familiar, so natural in his hand that he scarcely wondered what, why. . . . And read it through, to know how to file it away, before understanding that it was for him. It said that, in view of his recent bereavement and troubles, and also of the fact that he would in any case be retiring in the natural course very soon, the firm had decided that it would be easier for all concerned if he were to take his retirement from this date (Waggoner glanced at the date: it had been written a week after the murder charge); and that the firm would, without prejudice, pay him the sum of £0.95 per week, which was entirely *ex gratia,* since, as he knew, the firm had no pension fund; and it hoped that this sum would, added to his entitlement of benefits, assist him in his retirement. Elmwood, Braine & Hostace thanked Waggoner for his many years of loyal service, and were confident he would soon overcome his present difficulties.

'Blah! Blah blah!' Waggoner said aloud, impatient with the wording, and, distance having overcome his awe of Mr. Hostace, enjoying saying this disrespectfully into his face, as it were. He supposed that They knew and had worked out how much he would need to live, and that it would be forthcoming in some form or another. Perhaps the £0.95 would be enough to buy him a new pair of slippers? If not, he could save it up for a couple of weeks. And as for them being ready—it suddenly occurred to Waggoner in a brilliant flash of near-genius that if he were to walk backwards when he left the house, then stepped out of the slippers just inside the door: there they would be waiting for him, correctly positioned, correctly facing, when he came home again!

It wasn't really strange that he hadn't thought of this before, because there had always been someone else in the house, or at least likely to enter it, who would be inconvenienced by this. But now he had no one to think of, no one to consider but himself. Perhaps it wouldn't be so bad after all!

But still, going into the kitchen where the once shiny paper was bagging into blisters from the damp, wondering what he would eat, first pressing a ten-penny piece into the gas meter's grim slitted mouth, he thought with regret and some longing of those lost white-tiled corridors, the white plastic-topped tables, and the fried bread with margarine and fish paste that he'd had for supper in prison.

He remembered with nostalgia the Brussels sprouts (watery and rather tasteless, but to him exotic, since they were not in Agnes' culinary repertoire); the stewed steak, the puddings, sweet and gooey, the beds, hard but clean, with blankets like stiff-ironed card-board, smelling of chloride—which was acrid but not downright unpleasant. In fact it was a clean smell, with character, and Waggoner thought he could have grown to like it. He sighed, at paradise attained but lost again.

It was strange that the only words he had been allowed to say had been 'Not guilty': words he hadn't wanted to say, which had been untrue, and which everyone must have known weren't true; words that They, in the goodness of Their hearts and the mercifulness of Their justice, had forced him to speak.

Justice, after all, Waggoner supposed, must be done. They knew best, and if They had decided that Waggoner must live, he was Their responsibility.

The sentence, he supposed, was life.